To
all

THE SQUATTERS & OTHERS

A collection of short stories

by ROBERT NOTT

ISBN: 978-1-4834-3966-2 (sc)
ISBN: 978-1-4834-3965-5 (e)

Because of the dynamic nature of the Internet, any web addresses or links contained in
this book may have changed since publication and may no longer be valid. The views
expressed in this work are solely those of the author and do not necessarily reflect the
views of the publisher, and the publisher hereby disclaims any responsibility for them.

Any people depicted in stock imagery provided by Thinkstock are models,
and such images are being used for illustrative purposes only.
Certain stock imagery © Thinkstock.

Lulu Publishing Services rev. date: 10/28/2015

THE SQUATTERS

Office space was becoming a serious problem in the area and expansion by many firms was being hampered by it. In fact, Derek and Alan were so desperate for more space that they considered buying a private house with a view to endeavouring to obtain planning permission for change of use.

The location of their business was in an industrial area where, in the 1890s, masses of small terraced houses were built to accommodate the local workforce. But even these were selling at inflated prices. Although councils generally didn't mind the odd detached house being partly or even mainly used as office space, a converted terraced house could look completely out of place. This rather placed a damper on the plan but Derek and Alan continued to search for something suitable with a view to perhaps using half to let out to a member of staff as a flat and the rest, officially or otherwise, as an extended office.

Their search took them down all the side streets when they came across a detached house on its own in the dirtiest and most unpleasant part of the town. It was close to the banks of the Thames with a view out across the river but it was next to the rather smelly rubbish tip of a local factory. They could readily understand why nobody wanted to live there but found it hard to believe that the property could be so cheap – nearly half the price of something similar elsewhere in the town.

The house was advertised through local estate agents, Mayfield Estates. They informed Derek and Alan that the price was low because it had been on the market for some considerable time, with no takers to date. They passed over the keys to the prospective buyers and said "No, there is no need for us to go with you. We trust you; just bring back the keys when you've finished, when I think we can promise you that any reasonable offer will be accepted without too many arguments."

Derek and Alan couldn't believe their luck. They were all smiles. All smiles that is until they arrived at the property and opened the front door. They went inside. The front door slammed shut behind them; they were in complete darkness and felt shivers running down their spines as the temperature dropped by ten degrees.

"What the hell happened there?" asked Alan.

"Don't ask me" was the reply.

The pair searched desperately for the handle to open the nearest door. The door handle turned but there was obviously something wedged up behind the door because the more they pushed, the more the door resisted. Without warning, the pressure ceased, the door opened and they both crashed to the floor. The door slammed shut behind them.

There was very little light in the room. The windows were filthy and the stench over-bearing. What were originally net curtains, were torn, dirty rags full of cobwebs.

The two men looked at each other in the gloom. With a shaky voice, Alan said: "I guess we've got a fair old bit of work to do here. Better have a look at the rest of the place." He had hardly finished speaking when there was an almighty crash from upstairs, followed by a blood curdling scream and then – silence.

They looked at each other again without saying a word. After a few moments, Derek whispered: "Do we really need to go upstairs or have we seen enough?"

"I suppose we had better take a look – it can only get better! Hopefully! Have you got your torch with you?"

"Yes, luckily I brought one in case the electricity was turned off."

The pair walked out into the hall. Ahead of them was a staircase leading to the upper area of the house. Because of light coming only from the small torch, they took every step up the stairs carefully and with some trepidation. Each stair creaked, proving steeper than expected. Both men held on tightly to the banister rail. Halfway up, the rail came away from the wall and they found themselves tumbling downwards, landing in a heap at the bottom of the stairs.

"You all right, Alan?"

"I think so" came the reply.

Picking themselves up, they climbed the stairs again very slowly by virtually going up on 'all fours'. At the top was a small landing with one door in front of them and three others to the right. Not a sound anywhere.

They opened the door facing them and cautiously entered. It was another dark, filthy room; the smell was really dreadful. As they walked in, the door slammed shut and they heard footsteps on the stairs. From the small amount of light from the window, they could pick out a large wardrobe to their right and what appeared to be a kitchen chair. As they watched, the wardrobe suddenly swayed before crashing to the ground. The mirror on the wardrobe door broke into a million pieces and a very old but small version of a pirates' treasure chest fell off the top of the wardrobe.

There was the obvious urge to look inside but they continued towards the window to try to get more light to the room. Derek ran his gloved hand across the dirty glass in the window which enabled them to see out. Below was a small untended garden but there appeared to be a pathway leading away from the house across a small area of marshland towards the bank of the river. The ivy in the garden had grown up to the height of the window and was attempting to enter the room. They could see through the ivy that it partially concealed a ladder which was fixed to the outside wall – almost as if it were a fire escape of some description. Odd, but they thought little more of this at the time.

With the added light, their attention turned to an exceptionally large fireplace which had an iron grid running from one side to the other. A strange thing to have in a bedroom.

To the right of the fireplace was a built-in cupboard. Alan decided to take a look inside. As he cautiously opened the door, out fell a large cardboard box spilling the contents onto the floor. These consisted solely of skulls and thigh bones. These were, of course, the very bones used to provide the ashes from a cremation for passing to the relatives of a deceased person. They represented also the skull and crossbones on the flag of a pirate ship.

This raised the curiosity of the two men even more as to what was in the locked box which had fallen off the top of the wardrobe. They decided to take a look. It was easily opened because the screws holding the lock were rusted through. Slowly and carefully, Alan lifted the lid. Inside was a collection of hand-written notes, a few trinkets and virtually nothing more.

Suddenly, there was the sound of a cannon being fired which shook the whole building and the room was filled by a swirling cloud of grey dust. Simultaneously, from the next room came the screams of a woman in agony.

Alan and Derek had seen and heard enough; they made for the door which was locked tight. They tried to force it open but without success. They dashed towards the window, picked up the chair, smashed the glass and climbed down the ladder. They got halfway down when the steps on the ladder gave way and the whole thing collapsed on top of the couple who had fallen the rest of the way. They got up and just ran and ran; they couldn't get away from that place fast enough.

Eventually, they reached their car which they found covered with a slimy substance - just as though a large snail had climbed all over it. They got in the car and Alan attempted to start the engine; it wouldn't fire and absolute panic set in. He turned the ignition key again and again but nothing happened. Derek looked up towards the house and saw the ghastly figure of a woman dressed in black slowly making her way towards them. Her arms were outstretched beckoning them to come to her. He froze with fright but, suddenly, the engine started and they drove off at an alarming rate, tyres screaming.

"What the hell was that all about?" said Alan.

"Don't ask me!" replied Derek. "Let's get the hell out of here. I need a large whisky urgently!"

With the car still looking an absolutely terrible mess, they arrived at the estate agents. The manager greeted them with a smile saying: "Back so soon? Did you like it?"

"Like it? Have you ever been to that place?"

"Yes" replied the agent "But we don't go there these days."

"I should think not!" said Derek. "Why didn't you tell us what to expect?"

"Well, you know what kids are like. They are squatters. They've been there for some years now. It is rumoured that they broke into the place when the chap who owned it passed away. So that they could make a quick get-away if ever the need arose, it seems that they fixed a ladder up against the wall at the back. They planted some ivy to hide the ladder and that grew very quickly. They even went to the lengths of fitting a bigger fireplace in the back bedroom for cooking and to keep the place warmer.

"As you probably found out, they have the most elaborate of schemes to keep out potential buyers but you don't need to worry about that. Once you've bought it, we'll just chuck them out together with all their 'props'."

"Well, they really had us scared!"

"Yes, they would. It's surprising what you can do with a few stink bombs, party poppers and recordings. So, are you interested in buying? As I said, we'll help out by putting our security people in there to get the little blighters out before you move in to start work."

"We'll have to think about that but we just can't get over being so scared. Where the devil did they get all those skulls and bones?"

"That's easy. There used to be an old seventeenth century cemetery down the road which the council didn't know about until it started to excavate the land for possible building. That was when they dug up all those bones. They put them in cardboard boxes until they could be buried elsewhere but the kids pinched them before they could do so."

"That does make us look more than a bit silly. We'll almost certainly go ahead and make an offer. Thanks for being so helpful with the explanation."

The sale went through; the security people reported that the squatters had gone; Alan and Derek got workmen in to re-build the derelict house.

All went well until lunchtime on the first day when the workmen packed up their tools and left the site swearing that they would never return.

"That bl...y place is haunted! We are not going back in there. It was all right until this woman - that you could see right through - dressed in black just drifted into the room on which we were working screaming her head off and beckoning us to go to her. She then walked out through the front door which was locked solid! And every time we turned round we had to wipe this sticky stuff off all our tools. But to top it all, once we had finished plastering a wall, the whole building shook with the sound of this cannon going off and we had to do it again. We plastered the front room twice this morning and it still wants doing again. No, mate, we're not going back in there again. It's too spooky!"

Derek said "Well, we did tell you about squatters and their tricks."

"OK, you did tell us that there had been squatters in there but the people up the road told us that they had all moved out in a panic one night ten years ago! Apparently they were only there for one day."

Derek and Alan decided it would be better all round if they sold the place. But the question was: would they be able to find a buyer?

The problem was resolved when a few nights later the house was razed to the ground by fire. The fire brigade arrived to a burnt-out ruin. There were no signs of life but the sounds of screaming could be heard a mile away.

For Derek and Alan it was a happy scenario. The only decision for them to make was whether they should replace the large house and grounds with a purpose built office complex or simply sell the land to a local developer who wanted to build a block of flats. They made the decision to sell off the land and sit back with a handsome profit on the transaction. They would have to look elsewhere for their additional office space.

When completed, the flats looked absolutely marvellous with lovely views across the river and a beautiful landscaped garden. Without exception, people said that the flats were great but that strange noises and screams were heard all hours of the day and night. Some even confessed to hearing the sound of a cannon being fired. Thereafter,

'For sale' boards became plentiful and the flats were changing hands all the time.

"Wonder why that is?" Derek and Alan joked. "It must be those damn squatters!"

THE SQUATTERS (SEQUEL)

Paddy and Pam had both moved down from the north and had found employment in London. They were seeking accommodation in the form of a flat within commuting distance of the City. They were lucky enough to come across one advertised as virtually new and at a really knocked-down price.

Frankly, they were not interested in seeing the place as the plans were available on the net and it looked good, with marvellous views over the Thames. The price was at a give-away figure so what would be the point of getting a survey done? The flat was under a year old and carried a National House Building Council Guarantee. The location was right, the accommodation was what they wanted and the price was well under their budget figure. But, tongue in cheek, they made a lower offer than the advertised price and, much to their surprise, it was accepted in minutes. OK, so the neighbours might be something of a pain but Paddy was a big guy and would stand no nonsense in that respect.

The big day came when it was time to move in. They arrived in Paddy's car and were surprised to see 'For Sale' notices in the windows of every flat. That didn't particularly bother them because they had got good deal. Even if they had to sell the flat, how could they possibly lose money on it!

The trouble started within the first hour of their arrival. Door and windows in the block slammed and crashed shut continuously and there were footsteps running up and down the stairways. Paddy, who stood 6'3" and built like a rugby player, stalked out into the hallway and called out at the top of his voice: "Stop that bl...y racket!" and returned to the flat. Everything went eerily silent. After a few seconds came a woman's bloodcurdling screams and the sound of a cannon being fired. The latter shook the whole building and its contents – including their dining room table which had their unpacked crockery on the top of it.

Suddenly, a woman in black appeared through the closed front door and stopped. She stared at Paddy, raised her arms and beckoned him to come towards her. Paddy stepped towards her shouting; "Get out of here you nagging old bitch or I'll come and sort you out!" The woman disappeared just as suddenly as she had appeared – through the closed door.

"What the hell was that?" Pam was petrified.

"I don't know" said Paddy "But I am soon going to find out."

He went out into the hallway and rang the doorbell of their next door neighbour. He heard nothing for some time and eventually heard a timid voice say: "Who are you? Please don't hurt us."

"I won't be hurting you. I'm your new neighbour," replied Paddy.

The door opened slowly and a little old man stood there shaking with fear.

"Just how long has this been going on?" asked Paddy,

"Ever since we moved here. We don't get a minute's peace!"

"Can't the police help?"

"No, they won't even come here any more. They came a couple of times and met the old lady in black each time. They left running last time, only to find their police car covered in this slime that we seem to have all the time."

"Well, I can tell you now that I am going to sort this lot out," Paddy declared.

"Yes, but you've got to realise that this is supernatural stuff. It's not like just threatening a noisy neighbour. What do propose to do? If I can help I will because we can't sell this place at the moment and we are sick to death with worry over this going on all the time."

"I agree." Paddy was sympathetic. "But somebody somewhere must know what this is all about. Have you asked the local vicar if he could help with a drop of exorcism?"

"We've already tried that but last time he just ran for his life when the lady in black walked through him."

"I suppose it's worth a try."

Paddy did as he said and went to the library. He discovered that just up the River Thames from where they were living, prison ships had sailed for Australia. These ships, which sailed every three months from Greenwich, carried villains who had been a menace to society for carrying out such 'evil' deeds as stealing a loaf of bread when their families were starving.

Not unreasonably, some of the prisoners did all in their power to get off the ship while it was still in the Thames. But that was easier said than done. The river was fast flowing and was heavily polluted with rubbish and sewage. However, there was a fairly sharp bend in the river at Erith where the house was situated and the ships had to slow down for fear of running aground. It was then that some prisoners tried to make a break for it by jumping over the side and heading for the river bank. Over the years, many prisoners had attempted to jump ship and were drowned. Some were shot whilst swimming in the river or when they ran over the bank and were outlined against the sky line.

There had been an old widowed lady who lived in the detached house close to the banks of the river. She tried and succeeded in rescuing a lot of prisoners – some of whom were seriously injured by the gun fire from the ship. She kept them as long as she could but many died in her house and there was the constant fear of the army coming back to re-capture as many as they could. She made them comfortable upstairs in the back bedroom and had a ladder built on the back wall in case they needed a quick escape.

To dispose of the dead bodies, she buried as many as was possible in the garden; the remainder she burned on the big fire in the bedroom as she didn't know what else to do with them. She kept what few personal items the men had with them and placed them in a small chest which she kept out of sight on top of the wardrobe. The skull and thigh bones of each of those burnt were saved and placed in the small cupboard in case a relative had news of the escape and came wanting the remains of their loved ones. She gave them the first skull and thigh bone which came to hand from the box.

On one particular afternoon, as the ship slowed to make its passage round the bend in the river, several prisoners from the prison ship 'Freedom' jumped over the side. Some sank in the murky water; some were shot but others reached the shore and managed to clamber over the river bank to make their escape. It was a spring high tide so that the ship stood taller in the water. This enabled the ship's lookout to see the house quite clearly. Through his telescope, he could even see the old lady, dressed in black, standing at an upstairs window beckoning to the men she could see clambering over the bank to come to her home. The order on board ship was given to fire their cannon at the property. The very first and only shot hit her directly, blowing her dead and mangled body through the bedroom door and down the stairs.

Fearing for their lives, the escapees – both new and old - ran from the property leaving the dead woman with nobody to care for her remains.

This was the last time that there was an escape from any prison ship while it was in the Thames because the chains, which were previously removed from prisoners when the ship sailed, were retained until the ship left the river.

Paddy was not by any means a soft man but this tragic lady's sad story tore at his heartstrings. She did nothing but save men from a terrible fate. She came to be known as the *'black witch'* who haunted the property.

Although born a Roman Catholic in a small village outside Dublin, Paddy did not really regard himself as being a religious person. But he visited the local vicar and asked him to return to the property to hold a service dedicated to the work of the widow and to perform a figurative burial of her and the men who died whilst in her care.

The other residents willingly joined in the plan – anything to be able to live in peace in their flats. A full service was held in the garden and a plaque placed there in her memory. At the end of the service, there was an extremely loud sound of a cannon firing. The whole building shook. From an upstairs window, the black widow appeared with a smile on her face. Instead of beckoning people to come to her, she waved goodbye. All in the crowd waved back. She disappeared just as quickly as she had appeared.

Nothing was ever seen or heard of the lady again. Peace prevailed. But, once a year, on the anniversary of the date of the service, if you listen carefully, you can still hear the sound of a cannon being fired in the distance.

The Freezer

When Tim and Mary down-sized from their house to a flat at the coast, a lot of prized possessions just simply had to go – including their extremely large tub freezer which they had had for over ten years. It was always so full to over-flowing with food that the lid hardly closed. They were glad when their daughter said she would love to have it for this meant she could have the contents as well. Otherwise they would have been at a loss as to what to do with them.

Some three months earlier, Tim had acquired some really large Mediterranean prawns as fishing bait. They had been given to him by his neighbour, Malcolm, whose freezer had broken down. He told Tim to use them as bait as they had already de-frosted once and he was worried that they may be going-off.

Tim kept the prawns in a green plastic bag in the freezer and would take it with him when he went fishing. He let the prawns defrost on the beach before using them as otherwise he could not get the hook into them. When he got back home, he would re-freeze what remained of the bait until the next time he went fishing.

Two weeks after they moved into their new flat, Tim realised that his precious green bag was still in the freezer - which his daughter now had. So he rang her and explained that there was a green bag in the freezer. However, before he could tell her that it contained his fishing bait, his daughter interrupted him to say that they had eaten the Mediterranean prawns and that they were absolutely delicious!

They Sail Among Us!

Just below Maidstone on the River Medway is a lovely marina at a place called Allington. Its location is superb, being situated a couple of hundred yards from the first lock up the river. For a couple of hours on either side of high water, the lock can be opened which allows for an easy run down river, past Chatham, to some lovely and somewhat remote saltwater inlets close to Sheerness. These inlets also afford safe mooring for over-night stays before crossing the Channel.

Andrew kept his boat at Allington. He had planned a weekend fishing trip with two friends, Bob and Ron, in the autumn down river to an inlet called Stangate Creek where flounders and grey mullet were plentiful.

They were about to leave the marina around mid-afternoon on Saturday when another boat owner, Ian, asked if he and his wife could follow on behind in their boat. They had not made the trip before. Andrew agreed but stressed that, if they were held up as darkness fell, he would need a decent chart, echo sounder on board and a powerful light. Ian assured Andrew that he had the required equipment on board.

They left the marina in convoy. Andrew, however, was unaware that the chart Ian possessed was an old AA Book, which showed the entire length of the thirty-odd mile river Medway as being a mere two inches long; that Ian's echo-sounder didn't work and that his light consisted only of a handheld torch.

The journey went according to plan and the group entered Stangate Creek as the light started to fade. The party had travelled down with the fall of the tide which meant that, when they arrived at a suitable mooring, it was fairly close to low water. Andrew checked on the tide height and dropped the anchor in the deepest part of the creek to allow for a further fall of about three feet. He allowed ten fathoms (sixty feet) of anchor chain for the tide rise of around eighteen feet during the night. It was customary in that area for the anchor cable to be at least three times the depth of water.

The lads enjoyed a lovely meal, washed down with a bottle or three of wine; they went to bed at around 10.0 pm and slept soundly.

Come the next morning, Ian's boat were nowhere to be seen. As they couldn't get an answer from him on the radio, they guessed that he and his wife had gone back to the Marina.

The fishing on the Sunday morning turned out to be a waste of time: none of the three men had a single bite so, after an early lunch and a few beers, they decided to return to the Marina on the last couple of hours of the flood tide.

When they got back, there was no sign of Ian, his wife or the boat. What on earth could have happened to them? They shared their concern with the marina owner who decided to contact the coastguard.

It appeared that Ian had taken no account of the tide rise and, as a consequence, his anchor had simply lifted off the bottom during the night. The boat then drifted with the tide with the anchor hanging like a gigantic fish hook six feet below. It left Stangate Creek and drifted out into the middle of the very busy River Medway with its many oil tankers. The river at that point is nearly half a mile in width and has a depth of some fifteen fathoms. The tide took the boat five miles past the Isle of Sheppey and out into the heavy traffic of the Thames Estuary.

Just over a mile off Sheerness is the wreck of the famous 'SS Montgomery', a munitions ship which ran aground in 1944 during the Second World War. It still is a terrible hazard for shipping despite the fact that some of its structure is visible. For seventy years it has remained firm with its one thousand four hundred tonnes of explosives still on board. It is monitored twenty-four hours a day by port authorities and protected by a five hundred metres exclusion zone. Successive governments have wrestled with the problem of what to do with the wreck. If the vessel were to explode, it would probably flatten the whole of Sheerness!

Ian's drifting boat was spotted by a crew member on a passing tanker who reported the lack of seamanship to the coastguard. The authorities could not contact Ian as his radio didn't work as he and his wife slept on.

They were finally awoken by the sound of voices coming from the coastguard boat which had pulled up alongside their craft.

"Anybody on board?" was the first question they heard. Ian got out of bed and went out on deck.

"Yes, what's the problem?" he asked, rubbing his eyes and looking around him in utter amazement that they were not still in Sandgate Creek.

"Where the devil are we?"

"Well, sir, you are now in the Thames Estuary having passed through the exclusion zone around the 'SS Montgomery' and causing a great hazard to shipping. What on earth do you think you are doing?"

With much embarrassment, Ian explained that they had anchored in Stangate Creek the previous evening and that is all he could remember.

"I'm terribly sorry, officer but, as you will gather, the whole thing was outside my control. I would never dream of being a problem to a living sole. I can only guess that I must have wrongly calculated the depth of water in the Creek; – that must happen to people all the time."

"What's up, dear?" came the voice of Ian's wife from below deck. "Is something wrong?"

"It's OK, my love, it's just that our anchor failed to hold us and we have drifted several miles away from Stangate Creek. But this officer has gallantly saved our bacon by coming alongside to rescue us. Thank you once again, officer. Should we get the engine started and head back to our marina?"

Instead of getting a simple answer to his question, Ian received a dressing down from the coastguard which he would not forget in a hurry.

"You people who buy boats without knowing a thing about them are a complete and utter menace. The sooner they introduce a licence to handle a boat as they do in Australia, the better off we all shall be!

"You are lucky that this is your first offence. I'll let you off with a caution on this occasion but, before you go, I need your full details which will go on record. If you do a damn fool thing like this again, you'll be in trouble with a capital 'T'!" Get the anchor up on board, turn the boat around and we'll follow you up into the River Medway. After that you will be on your own. Just watch your step and stick to the 5 knot limit once you have passed Chatham."

Back at the Marina, Ian thought the whole episode rather funny. His only comment was:

"If I had woken at my normal time on a Sunday morning, we could have had a nice bottle of red with our lunch in Calais!"

The reality was, of course, that it was more likely his small boat would have been sunk by the wash of one of the many large container ships or passenger ferries operating in that area - probably resulting in loss of life.

Indeed, it could have been 'goodbye' to the town of Sheerness and its inhabitants if his anchor had caught on the wreck as it passed so close to it.

Suffice it to say, nobody at the marina shared Ian's humour. On the contrary, his lack of responsibility filled every boat owner with horror. Nobody ever agreed to his accompanying them again and, within months, he left the marina permanently for pastures new.

Fair Cop

The plot couldn't have been much easier. It fact, it was fool-proof. The three close friends, Tony, John and Alan, had seen the horse they wanted and were determined it would be theirs by fair means or foul. But their offer to buy it was rejected out of hand because the owner said he needed all of the horses he had. They decided that they would simply take it.

On reflection, it might have been better had they given more thought to their proposal before taking the action they did. But they felt the matter was urgent and they could not foresee any difficulties.

The horse was quite small, one of eight kept in a large wooden building to the rear of the owner's house close to the local park, away from mainstream traffic. They had seen the owner place the horses there and had seen also the large gap in the woodwork of the building caused by one of the bottom planks having fallen off at ground level thereby making access a simple matter. As the nails were rusty, they could easily lever off a few more planks.

It would involve a two mile walk from where they lived. This meant they would leave no evidence. They would take their cart with them so it would a simple matter to walk there and bring the animal home with the cart.

They were impatient to get the job done; they agreed to set off from their homes at eight o'clock the following morning.

Everything went according to plan – although the two miles walk seemed more like five! They had taken with them a large screwdriver with which to lever off the planks of the building.

Reaching their destination just before nine o'clock, they approached the building containing the horses from the rear so that they could not be seen from the house where the owner lived.

They carefully removed the next to bottom plank but soon realised that from the position of the horses and their height they would need to remove a further four planks in order to gain complete access. The horses had their backs to the opening so a bit of manoeuvring would be necessary. It was a good job that the horses were small otherwise they would have had to remove the complete back of the building!

With something of a struggle, the three pulled the nearest horse backwards through the hole when there was a tremendous crash. The horse had fallen back on them knocking them to the ground and causing complete chaos amongst the other horses. Before they could consider their best retreat they found the owner staring down at them. They recognised him immediately and he them.

Needless to say, he was not pleased. He was a big but gentle man. He rang the police on his mobile, who arrived promptly as they were on another case of theft at a nearby factory.

Police Sergeant Blewitt was a kindly man. Everybody in the small area where they lived regarded him highly - he stood for no nonsense from hooligans or others who thought they could do just as they liked.

Their hearts sank when he arrived – especially when he addressed all three of them by their first names.

"And just what do you think you are doing?" he asked them in a gruff voice.

John, who was of a nervous disposition, was on the verge of tears. The other two didn't know where to look and just gazed down at their feet. The game was up and they would have to face the consequences.

The sergeant turned to the owner and asked him if he wished to press charges. There was an immediate sigh of relief from all three when the man said "No, nothing's missing. I can soon nail back the planks, so I'll just leave you to deal with the matter as you see fit." The horse was put back with the others.

The three were driven back to Tony's home in the police car. Although Sergeant Blewitt knew there were to be no charges, he wasn't having this type of thing going unpunished. He made phone calls to the homes of the other culprits. Their families agreed to join the group rather than having to trample down to the police station.

The three explained to everybody that they had offered the owner all their available cash – their total pocket money of £2.50. He thanked them but said he needed all eight of the merry-go-round horses to provide children's entertainment for the charity he ran every bank holiday. Sergeant Blewitt gave the three a mild but firm dressing down. The parents supported Sergeant Blewitt on this and banned their six-year-olds from television and their game stations for a week.

Excalibur

To say that Bill Johnson, the local Manager for a large insurance company, was committed to golf would probably be the understatement of the year and yet his rather frail and bent body from birth was not designed for such a pursuit.

The slight curvature of his spine meant that, when he addressed the ball, his left shoulder was some six inches higher than his right. He overcame the natural stiffness in his shoulders by swinging his club in a circular motion above his head before driving off at every tee. Although this seemed to give him the necessary relief, it did little to reassure his fellow players who ducked automatically as the club came in their direction.

Leeds Castle was a super venue. It had a small but intriguing golf course with the first hole played as a dog-leg around the lake. The more experienced players could, of course, hit the ball across the water to land close to the green.

It was a bitterly cold day in February with an icy wind blowing from the north-east and Bill was wearing a pair of thick woollen gloves before changing those for proper golfing gloves. Whilst pursuing his usual warm-up at the first tee, the club slipped from his hands and headed towards the middle of the lake.

Some said that a hand appeared from beneath the water, seized the clubs as it fell, held it high for a moment, with a voice exclaiming "Excalibur" before disappearing with the club into the depths – but the appearing and disappearing hand may have been added later after a few drinks at the bar.

Bill's only concern was what he would put on the insurance claim form to his company for a new golf club.

Buoy Ahead

Andrew's dad, Harry, kept a boat at Herne Bay in Kent. He went out fishing once a month with a few friends. Andrew was invited to go along to take part in his very first fishing competition. This was being organised by the Heron Angling Society.

This particular resort had some good fishing grounds. The only problem was that you could only realistically launch and recover a boat for two hours on either side of high water. If you missed the gap, then you could get stuck on the sand waiting for the next high tide - some twelve hours later.

The trip was nearly cancelled because of a heavy sea mist but, as the weather forecast indicated that it would soon be clearing, it was decided that it could go ahead.

In the autumn, the Weir Bank is a favourite spot for fishing because it is home to a variety of fish, including the thornback skate. It is situated about a mile or so off shore and is easily located by boat. You simply line up the church spire in the centre of the town with the end of the pier. The boat's echo sounder would indicate the shallower water of the bank on arrival there. It should take about ten or 15 minutes to arrive – depending on the tide and the roughness of the sea.

Andrew wanted to prove his worth so he asked if he could steer the boat. His dad agreed. Looking carefully, the end of the pier and the church spire could just about be seen which enabled him to set the course by the compass. There was an additional visual aid in the form of a large mooring buoy situated about halfway along the passage. The mist started thickening, so one of the party sat in the bow watching out for the buoy - just to make sure that the boat had not drifted too much with the wind and tide.

After a few minutes, the call was 'Buoy ahead'. Great, they were on course! Some ten minutes later the call was 'Buoy ahead'. Andrew's dad grabbed the chart and, no, there was no second buoy marked. Still, it might be a temporary one placed there by the local professional fisherman to mark a crab basket. It was a bit large for a marker buoy but it was decided to proceed on the same course. The boat continued on its way for a few more minutes when the voice rang out 'Buoy ahead'.

Harry went to the compass and there next to it was Andrew's radio switched on but with the sound turned down. When the radio was removed, it showed that the boat was on the wrong course. The battery in the radio was interfering with the compass and the boat was going round in circles. They attempted to follow the original course for a while but the fog was now as thick as pea soup. They had absolutely no idea where they were.

As the fog was scheduled to clear, it was decided to just drop anchor and wait for that to happen. They baited up their hooks and started fishing.

Although the depth of water showed clearly enough that they were not on the Weir Bank, the fishing was not bad. Everybody on board caught a few fish.

Eventually the fog did clear and they could see several other boats some two or three hundred yards away. Quite obviously they were on the Weir Bank but it was not worth changing location that late in the day and, after all, they had a reasonable catch.

Time came for them to go back in order not to miss the tide. Their return was uneventful. They secured the boat and made their way to the competition tent with the bag containing their fish. They were the first to 'weigh-in' and they were quite delighted when the scales measured 19-1/2 lbs. That would make a nice dinner for them all when they got back home.

They waited to see what the others caught and wondered if they would be collecting one of the prizes.

The next boat in was smaller than theirs. They just couldn't believe their ears when the judge announced a total weight of 56 lbs. This included a Weir Bank's skate at 9 lbs and a dozen of the largest flounders they had ever seen.

Boat after boat weighed in good catches and the five went home feeling more than a little disappointed. They could have done much better if they had reached the Weir Bank. They felt like throwing Andrew's radio in the sea but, instead, he got a pat on the back for his contribution and nobody mentioned his radio when inviting him to the next outing. Without being told, he never took it again.

Tibia & Fibula Meals Up For Grabs

The various excursions offered by the cruise company were not up to much. They were expensive and didn't represent value for money. In fact, most of the passengers were getting off the ship and taking one of the hundred or so taxis plying for trade. The cost was often less than half of the same trip by coach - and didn't include the compulsory stop-offs to buy junk which nobody wanted at over-priced stores.

The passengers seated at the same table for dinner every evening resolved to form their own group. When they left the ship at the next port, they hired an eight-person open mini-bus to pay a visit to Purple Heart Beach. This was renowned as being a most beautiful, sandy bay and well worth a visit.

They enjoyed a great lunch at a restaurant suggested by their driver. He sat dining modestly with a few other drivers at the restaurant's expense while the group had a table to themselves. After lunch they went on to their destination

Purple Heart's beach was really something to see with its tropical style palm trees growing from the sand. It was remarkably quiet for such a beautiful place and the ocean was a crystal clear blue-green colour at a temperature of a warm bath.

The men decided to go in for a swim while the ladies did a bit of sun-bathing. About two hundred yards out into the bay, there were half a dozen local lads who were having fun on a raft. The menfolk decided to swim out to join them.

They swam for a hundred yards or so and came across a rope just below the surface of the water. Quite obviously, it was a contraption of some sort or another used by the local fishermen to catch crabs and lobsters.

When they arrived at the raft, they teased the lads telling them jokingly that they owned the raft and that the lads had to be thrown off. What followed was absolutely hilarious; the boys and men alternated in climbing back on the raft and pushing off those on it. It was easy for the boys who appeared to have boundless energy but the men soon became tired and they all sat in a line with their legs dangling in the water. Everybody had a great time. Almost immediately they were joined on the raft by the father of one of the boys who had been watching all the fun and decided to swim out to join them.

He said that it was not a good idea to sit with their legs in the water because it was dangerous to do so – particularly at that time of day. He said that he was more than a bit surprised when he saw the men swim over the shark net to reach the raft. Had they not seen the sign farther up the beach? He said "It's fine for the boys because they always keep a watchful eye open for the sharks - which they know enter the bay seeking food at almost set times each day."

Not only did the men react immediately by pulling their feet out of the water but suddenly found it was time for them to go back to the beach: "Because the ladies had been left on their own for too long already!"

Olympic swimming speeds were shattered as the men swam for the shore!

Your Country Needs You

Terry's step-mother was a very tall, slim woman. She had three other sons of her own who were much younger than Terry. She did not hide the fact that she disliked him intensely and he her. His father had married again when Terry's real mother died.

Bob lived just a few houses away in the same road. He and Terry were great friends. Funnily enough, they really had little in common and they even went to different schools. That didn't stop them meeting up whenever they could simply to enjoy each other's company.

When they left school, both obtained employment in the City of London but with different companies. They travelled up to London to work by train together every day.

Terry could best be described as a natural bachelor; although only 17 years of age, he loved his pint, always had a pipe hanging out of his mouth and the latest joke was never far from his lips. Bob was more of a family man and had a regular girlfriend.

It was 1951, when young men of 18 were 'called up' for a period of two years National Service. Terry's father had been a sergeant in the army during World War 2 and he reminded Terry and Bob regularly of their fast approaching commitment to serve their 'King and Country'.

In reality, Terry was quite looking forward to the excuse to leave home but the lingering problem for him was that they would almost certainly be drafted into the Army where, as Terry put it, "You can bet your last dollar we shall finish up in the infantry." Frankly, this didn't appeal to either of them because international conflicts involving

British troops were commonplace at the time. The Korean War has just finished but there were still problems in Malaya.

It was a cold, miserable and misty February day that Terry came up with the startling news that he had a plan which simply 'just could not fail'.

"I read only this morning that the RAF are looking for young men to train as pilots. Entry could be six months before the normal National Service age of 18, so we could sign up straight away. It would mean signing-on for a four year term but just think of the advantages. We would be officers, receive much higher pay and, at the end of the four years, we would pocket a gratuity of £500."

Bob wasn't that keen on the idea. "I've got no real wish 'to risk life and limb' by pretending I'm a bird and flying aeroplanes" he replied "But I must confess that £500 – well, that's something different. Let's go for it!"

So the date was fixed for their assessment at the RAF station of Hornchurch in Essex. They would have to undertake aptitude tests and face a tough medical examination. They were both staggered at the huge number of young men arriving at the same time for the same purpose. When they sat at the desks provided, Terry counted 92 would-be flyers.

Following the tests were personal interviews when success or failure would be announced. As these were done alphabetically on family name, Terry was interviewed some time before Bob. Everybody went in one door but left by another.

Bob was advised that he had been successful in his application and he signed the necessary paperwork. He just couldn't wait to catch up with Terry.

"Well, I made it, Terry. How did you get on?"

Terry was very distraught and in a quavering voice said: "Out of all that lot, only two people were accepted for pilot training – and I wasn't the other one."

"Oh, golly, Terry. What are you going to do?"

"Well, I just got to get away from home so I signed on for eight years as an airframe fitter. But, don't worry, Bob, I'll probably be working on the plane that you are flying -so everything will work out in the end."

Bob was not convinced but said he agreed with Terry's thoughts just to keep his spirits up.

In reality, Bob had misgivings about the whole thing. He had no particular interest in joining the RAF other than the fact that he and Terry would be together and, of course, to enjoy the eventual financial rewards.

Just one month later, both were ordered to report to RAF Cardington in Bedfordshire and they decided to go together using the travel warrants provided.

When they arrived at the railway station, Terry found himself in receipt of a third class ticket while Bob's was first class. That didn't matter too much; they just sat together in a third class compartment.

When they arrived at Cardington railway station, they were met by the RAF police. Terry was directed to climb into the back of a waiting lorry while a taxi was hailed for Bob. This was not quite what the two of them had planned. But they had agreed previously that, if they got separated, they would meet up in the NAAFI that evening. There was bound to be a NAAFI on the camp; there always was.

This plan worked; they had a sandwich together and left agreeing to meet the following night at the same venue. But this was not to be for, on leaving the NAAFI, Bob was stopped by the RAF police and advised that he could not socialise with enlisted men.

The next day, Bob was taken to RAF Cranwell for training as an Officer Cadet Pilot while Terry was posted to Dumfries for his six weeks of 'square bashing' - the slang term for learning how to march and handle a rifle – before learning his trade.

Within twelve months, Bob was medically discharged from the RAF with tachycardia – rapid heartbeat - and shortly afterwards married the girl he loved. They moved out of the immediate area in which they had lived.

Terry served eight most unhappy years as an airframe fitter. Bob heard later that Terry had married a widow with three children and moved to Devon.

The two friends, who were so close from childhood, were destined never to meet or speak again after their separation that day in Cardington.

The Arsonists (Sequel to Your Country Needs You)

Bob arrived at Cranwell. He found himself one of the youngest cadets. Many were already in the RAF but had requested a transfer to aircrew. There were sergeants, corporals and even officers from varying RAF trades but these were all temporarily stripped of their ranks and became Officer Cadets. As a Cadet, you were entitled to be addressed as 'Sir' by other ranks but the training sergeants and corporals made the word sound more of a curse than a title.

Cranwell was in two distinct sections. There was the College for career officers. This was the RAF's equivalent of the Army's Sandhurst. Career officers would be based there for up to two years and would leave with the rank of Flying Officer.

There was, in addition, what the RAF called a 'Training Wing' for the initial training of pilots and navigators. Cadets were billeted in a series of barrack huts which were baking hot in the summer and freezing cold in the winter.

The course consisted of three months of intense training in drill, forecasting the weather associated with various cloud formations, learning the Morse Code to a respectable standard, and navigating a plane from one place to another on a map. During this period, no leave was permitted. Most found it tough going - but particularly so to those new to the RAF, like Bob. He had never held a rifle yet alone assembled one from a 'pile of bits' – as he put it. Those who could not cope were removed from the course with papers marked 'LMF' which stood for 'lack of moral fibre'.

In addition to those who left voluntarily, after six weeks, half the cadets were released as not being up to the required standard. At the end of three months, half of the remaining cadets were advised that they would not be proceeding to the next stage.

All this led to competition between the cadets which, in itself, provided the occasional light moment. It seemed that the pass mark was always the major factor. On one occasion, the cadets were undertaking practice parachute jumps in an aircraft hangar. One of the cadets enquired as to how many successful parachute jumps a cadet had to undertake from a plane.

"All of them, sir!" was the sergeant's reply. Laughter all round except on the red face of the enquirer.

So, to reach the final 'passing out' parade, the successful Cadets had much to celebrate. They were automatically elevated to the rank of Acting Pilot Officer and posted to Flying Training Schools. That stage would consist of training in such non-important factors as actually starting the engine of a plane, getting it off the ground and landing it in one piece.

It was part of RAF philosophy not to inform the newly appointed officers in advance as to the destination for their next course of training. It was recognised, however, that the usual posting would be to either Southern Rhodesia or Alberta in Canada. In reality, the secrecy was something of a farce. Bob received a great coat while the chap in the next bed was provided with short sleeve shirts and shorts. Guess who was going where!

The last day at the Training Wing was by custom a boisterous affair. After three months of great pressure there needed to be a release valve. Each year the antics of the cadets became more outrageous. Having first removed all their personal belongings, hoses were run into the barrack huts to drench the walls and floors, whilst the windows would be blackened with boot polish. The new cadets arriving would face the task of cleaning up the mess. This was literally par for the course. It was accepted by all as being reasonable behaviour. The inspecting officer on making his rounds to see the incoming cadets, would simply step over the hose pipes, ignore the imperfections and invite the new cadets to "Carry on please". That was for the first day only! The next day the barrack rooms would have to be 'spick and span'.

The new cadets were due to arrive just before lunch and the outgoing officers would leave later in the day having seen the fun. So, whatever had to be done needed to be undertaken early in the morning immediately after the outgoing men had packed their bags. These were then placed in the departure area. The important task of watching over the luggage fell on Bob - who was thus prevented from joining in the fun.

Cadet Charles Maddison came up with a bright idea. "Why don't we stuff a few blankets down the chimneys of the barrack huts? When the new lot arrive, the first thing they will do is to light the stoves because of the cold weather. Smoke everywhere; lots of fun!"

Well, there were plenty of volunteers to climb on the roofs and do just that. However, things did not quite go according to plan. The barrack rooms filled with smoke all right when the fires we lit but flames were seen coming out of the chimneys. The local fire engine was called and the fires were contained. From the black smoke everywhere, it was felt that the huts were likely to be out of use for the foreseeable future.

The Wing Commander, far from inviting everybody to "Carry on please", was absolutely furious and summoned all the new officers to the parade ground immediately.

"Whose bright idea was it to flood the huts with hoses? Those men responsible, take one pace forward." To a man, the whole wing stepped forward. He then asked for those who had blackened the windows with boot polish to step forward. Again, the whole Wing did so.

"Right then. Whose bright idea was it to set fire to the barrack huts by stuffing blankets down the chimneys?"

When Arnold looked round, he found that he had been the only one to have moved. The others were glued to the spot. The Wing Commander took one look at the rather frail, somewhat pathetic 5'6" figure of Arnold and realised that he could hardly have climbed on all five roofs on his own. Obviously, the new officers were not an honourable lot.

Without thinking at all of the consequences, the Wing Commander ordered that everybody would be punished by seven days confinement to camp. He was stalking off in high dudgeon when he was brought to an abrupt halt by one of the new officers, Alec Robinson.

"May I just point out, sir, that the travel arrangements and warrants are all dated for today for the removal of the new officers to their various destinations abroad? In addition, if they were to remain, there is simply not the accommodation to cater for both the outgoing officers and the incoming cadets."

Robinson thought he was being very clever to point these things out. In reality, all it did was to make the Wing Commander look a complete and utter fool in front of all his men. It also placed him in a difficult position. How could he punish the men and, at the same time, cope with the problems the punishment created. He left without saying a word or dismissing the men.

Nothing happened for an hour while the men waited patiently still in their places on the parade ground. They kept looking at their watches as travel time approached. Then came the announcement over the tannoy "Travel will proceed as planned but take note that the Wing Commander will be preferring charges for arson on all men in the Wing. The matter will be dealt with at the highest possible level. Careers in the service will undoubtedly be at stake."

The new officers left the camp. Each man worrying seriously about the charge hanging over him. Were it not for that idiot, Robinson, the chances were that they would have been allowed to go on their way with nothing more said. In any case the Wing Commander had not said to which camp they were to be confined. But Robinson's big mouth had really dropped them in it!

But nothing more was ever again heard about the incident. The Wing Commander had taken his revenge as the new officers waited and waited to know their fate. Punishment enough – especially when it was found that, after a clean-up, there was no real damage. The huts were occupied that very same day when the inspecting officer invited the occupants to "Carry on please."

The Secret Ingredient

Brian's mother was a dead ringer for Popeye's Olive Oyle. She was a tall, skinny and flat-fronted lady who had an almost completely round face with her hair drawn back into a bun.

She had an absolutely packed kitchen every Saturday morning. Kids from the neighbourhood were there to sample her absolutely scrumptious rock cakes.

Into the bowl went the flour, the eggs, the milk, the sugar, currants and the butter. She then stood on a chair and took something from an unlabelled packet which was on the top shelf of her kitchen cupboard. She stirred and stirred the mixture for a long time before it was finally dispatched to the heated oven.

All eyes were glued though – not on the mixing bowl with its obvious special secret ingredient – but on the cigarette permanently dangling from between her lips. The children watched the cigarette with its ever-increasing length of ash. It would seem that not even her smoker's cough could be seen to dislodge it. But, suddenly, it was gone. Gone where? Nobody could see how she performed this trick. So they watched patiently as the next lot of ash grew and grew but it, too, vanished without trace before their very eyes.

The mystery deepened; just where did the ash go? Nobody knew.

The other mystery which remained was that secret ingredient from the top shelf which gave the delicious rock cakes their truly different taste and their unusual grey colour.

Foggy Day

Golf for Jack and Bob was a weekly event. It has to be said that they were not the best players in the club. In fact, if the truth were known, they were among the very worst. But they were 'passed their sell-by date' age-wise and enjoyed their outing. Not unnaturally, they failed to acquire a formal club handicap from the Club but were proud to boast that they were club members. They remained silent when discussions turned to handicaps and there were times when they resorted to going to the bar to obtain another drink when it was turn to disclose theirs.

They preferred playing in the winter months rather than the summer. There were fewer people willing to face the bitter cold of playing golf on the top of a hill where the club was situated. The reality was that there were fewer people also to complain about how slow they were going round the course.

But, come wind, rain or shine, they were there as soon as it was light. They proffered a variety of unlikely explanations to their wives who wondered why on earth they were crazy enough to be going out when the weather was so bad.

Came this particular day, the fog was so thick that it was too dangerous to even drive to the golf club yet alone play. Their wives expressed their usual concern but they were assured that "This fog is very localised and the road will be completely clear within a hundred yards or so."

But when they arrived at the golf club an hour later, having hugged the kerb for some five miles, it was worse than ever. They had to ask to be directed to the first tee and the club secretary told them they must be mad to even consider playing. "Why don't you wait for an hour or two" he suggested but they were having none of that.

So they got to the first tee and, from memory, they knew that the green was situated roughly in "That direction" said Jack pointing with his club. Charlie moved a step closer so that he could actually see where Jack was pointing.

Jack, who at the age of 81 was the elder of the two, came up with the bright idea that they should use yellow balls. They had played in thick snow two weeks earlier when he had recommended that they use red balls. These had completely disappeared in the five inches of snow which covered the course. On that occasion they lost six balls on the first hole which prompted them to abandon the game and settle for a cooked breakfast in the club house.

But they were confident that the yellow balls would be capable of being seen in the fog - provided they could hit them straight down the fairway. That, in all fairness, was something of a rarity.

Very gingerly, they drove off from the first tee not attempting to hit the ball as hard as was their usual custom. They trudged along in what they considered to be a straight line. After 150 yards, there was still no sign of their balls and they feared a repetition of their exploits in the snow. But they walked on and, much to their surprise, found both balls had travelled around 175 yards. This was almost double their usual distance. Prompted by this success, they actually completed all eighteen holes and found that their scores were the best ever.

They were so proud of their achievement that they showed their cards to the Club Secretary enquiring whether they might count towards an official handicap. But he was having none of that and politely suggested that they follow the procedure clearly outlined in the club rules.

Needless to say, they opted not to exercise this right. The following week they were back on form playing to their usual dreadful standard, with voices behind them asking "May we play through?" Which is golfing parlance for permission to go ahead of them because they were taking too long.

High Flyer

Ted's parents were always overly-protective of their young son. He had been an apprentice fitter and turner resulting in his enlistment for National Service being delayed by three years. His parents were concerned that two years in the army might not be good for their lad, so they managed to gain him exemption by getting him a job in the merchant navy. Many other parents did the same.

He came home more frequently than most might have expected but he always looked so very splendid in his dress uniform. It was obvious to all that he was an officer. True there were no medals as such but his exploits indicated that some honour was imminent. In any event, although he refused point blank to discuss it, his white lanyard must have meant that he was an aide to somebody or another of very senior rank.

He always brushed aside with an air of confidentiality any questions as to his rank and exactly what he did. Anyone who persevered always finished up engrossed in a tale of exploits in some exotic part of the world.

As the years passed and his parents left the area, people saw less and less of Ted. It was assumed that his original five year engagement had become a life-time career in a far off place. He was virtually forgotten by all who had known him previously.

Forgotten, that is, before Mike appeared on the scene. He, too, had been in the merchant service for years. He would recount stories of what he did and of the people he had met on his travels. One of his stories made mention of a suave, young third engineer named Ted. As it happens, he was from their area. For many a year – and still was - an engineer on the Woolwich Free Ferry which carried cars the 200 yards across the River Thames. It appears that the engineers always wore a lanyard. This held a whistle which was blown to signal the closing of the gates when the ship was about to sail.

The Tricks of the Trade

Tony was not what one might describe as a great scholar but he 'scraped home' in every subject except maths. In fact, he managed to fail his examination in maths no less than three times. He felt he was good in the subject but results proved quite conclusively otherwise.

On leaving school, Tony joined a marine insurance company in the 'City'. One of his monthly tasks was to go through the sales ledger and bring out a balance on each of the 150 accounts listed. These balances had to be added together to give a final sum. This was then compared to that brought out by the firm's accountant by other means.

During the first six months, not once did the figures agree and Tony got completely frustrated. It was not that after six months he got the sums right, it was just that they transferred the job to somebody else in the department who, of course, got it right first time.

Funnily enough, they did not furnish Tony with other work to replace the accounting side. The truth of it was that the company was never very busy and the staff did little. This was because its main occupation consisted of dealing with long-outstanding marine claims which, for a variety of reasons, often took ten years to settle.

Two of the senior staff members who were both nearing retirement did virtually nothing other than smoke their pipes and talk about tobacco. They grew the tobacco themselves and added various ingredients, like honey, which they had experimented with over the years. Both of them starting to make their own tobacco when they served together in the RAF. At that time, in order to get the leaves pressed to their satisfaction they placed the mix under a board and arranged for a pilot to run his bomber wheel on to it. Obviously they had as little to do in the RAF as they did working in the City.

Their tobacco was very strong indeed. They used to enjoy getting visitors to the office to try some. They watched their victim's face with delight when they took their first puff and realised how strong it was. Many turned almost green.

The lack of work left Tony with much time on his hands. This resulted in his spending ages talking to the company's Sergeant. These Sergeants were largely ex-army types who provided a most useful messenger service. Most of the larger companies employed at least one. They acted virtually as local postmen carrying documents from one company to another by hand. With businesses being so close to one another in the City, it was much easier, reliable and quicker than using the national postal service.

Most of these messengers had additional responsibilities which took a variety of forms. Some dealt with the storage of larger documents in the cellars, filing or handling the postal service at the end of each day.

Tony's Sergeant was called Phil Norris. He was a very smartly dressed individual in his late 50's who had been with the Company for some years. He was very punctual, reliable and helpful. Like everybody else, he did little but, strange at it may seem, he always seemed fully occupied. It was part of his duties to answer the telephone when the receptionist was otherwise occupied. Some of his conversations were not always easy to follow.

One day, Tony asked Phil what he actually did. Phil confided in him that he ran his own insurance agent's business from their office. His clients would ring him there and he spent much time in going backwards and forwards to insurance companies in the City placing his own clients' business.

The more that Phil said about his activity, the more Tony learnt about the insurance business generally. He found it all so fascinating. He spent much time learning the many 'tricks of the trade' from Phil who was quite obviously a very clever man. He had a business address in the City with all the associated expenses like rent and rates, electricity, heating, telephone calls, postage, the use of a typewriter and notepaper all supplied free of charge by his employers. No wonder he always had a smile on his face.

There was one thing which Phil said that Tony would never forget: "The control of money is the most important thing for every business. Never lose sight of that fact!"

Tony left the Company when he was 'called up' for military service but, immediately this was finished, he again sought employment in insurance. After some years of working for a leading insurer, he eventually opened his own insurance brokerage.

His business grew and grew and was eventually to become one of the largest independent brokerages in the county. He had an ever-increasing number of staff. This would involve him spending much time in teaching them many of the 'tricks of the trade' which he had learnt some 35 years earlier from Phil Norris. He taught them how to calculate the most complicated of percentages without resource to pencil and paper.

Well, believe it or not, over the years Tony gained quite a reputation for his teaching expertise – particularly in the field of finance and mathematics. Indeed, when Tony retired, he was considered to be something of an expert on Cash Flow Forecasting. He spent much time lecturing on the subject to businessmen – when he would often quote the words of Phil relating to the control of money.

So that represented a complete swing of the pendulum for the guy who failed maths three times but who had learnt practical maths as one of the many 'tricks of the trade' from his mentor, Sergeant Norris.

Christchurch Clock

The town of Erith in North West Kent is just 14 miles from central London. It is situated on the south bank of the River Thames and had settlements dating back to the 1st century AD. The name is thought to have been derived from a word meaning 'muddy harbour' or 'gravelly landing place'. It was famous for the fitting-out there of Henry VIII's ship, the *"Henri, Grace a Dieu"*.

Because the ground rises steeply, clearly seen from the river itself is the large 'Christchurch' clock. The main face on the clock looks out over the Thames. It is said that, in olden days when sailing ships had not the electronic equipment of modern vessels, mariners always checked their time with the clock on passing up or down the river.

But like most mechanical things, the clock went wrong and, for some years, the hands were stuck at 11.30 and the chimes remained silent.

Church Warden, Tom Beadle, was chatting one day to Bill Kendall who was a local shopkeeper. "When we get an estimate for repair of the clock we start fund-raising but, by the same we have actually got the money, the cost of repair has doubled and we have to start all over again. What money we had collected is spent on other major problems. I don't know how we shall ever get the clock repaired."

Bill asked why they didn't borrow the money from the bank but the answer came that the church was already overdrawn and the bank wouldn't come up with any more funds. The Bishop had also been approached but his reply was "I have better things on which to spend the little money I have than repairing a clock." So that was dead in the water too.

Having pondered on the problem, Bill went back to see Tom with his suggestion.

"Why don't you get an estimate for repair and give instructions for the work to be put in hand. Immediately the cost is known, I'll divide this between ten members of the local Rotary Club who have agreed to lend the money to the church without interest. You can then get cracking with your fund-raising and repay the money as and when you can."

Tom thanked Bill profusely and said he would put the matter to the church council. The offer was gratefully accepted. The estimate was obtained and the work put in hand. There was a lot to do and most of this involved the use of scaffolding. It was estimated that, getting somebody to do the job on a part-time basis to save money, it would take about three months to complete.

During that time dances and social programmes were put in hand to raise the money and they had actually got the lot before the work was even finished. This meant that the loans were never required and everybody was happy.

Well, nearly everybody! Brenda had bought a rather pleasant house next to the church a year or two earlier. She was always saying what a peaceful place it was to live. Well, it was until the bell started to chime every fifteen minutes both day and night.

"It was bad enough having the church bells rung every Sunday morning without this lot on top" was her complaint to the vicar and the local press.

Eventually, the problem was resolved by not having the clock chime after 9.0 o'clock at night and not starting again until 9.0 am the following morning.

Special Breeds' Farm

The land on which the special breeds' farm was situated was owned by the Local Council. It had run the farm itself for some years with its own employees. But, as the Chief Executive Dick Griffiths had said at a meeting of interested parties "Organising special events and undertaking changes in the stock have proved to be most onerous. That is why we have decided to lease out the farm to people with more expertise. However, we are prepared to give it financial support in any way we can to ensure its continued success."

Two young, local entrepreneurs, Tony and Bertie, had been at the meeting and decided to purchase the lease from the Council. They had been looking for a local project to develop and impressed the Council with their ideas. They were accepted as being suitable for the job and the lease was signed in the summer.

They could not have worked harder to expand the business into something worthwhile. It was quickly proving itself to be a useful asset to the community. Parents could take their children for interesting and educational visits. The Birds of Prey Section and the Snake Pit were particularly attractive to both young and old alike.

The special programme for September Bank Holiday Monday had attracted literally hundreds of people. There were clowns mixing with the crowds, a small group of musicians playing popular melodies and many prizes for the children. They were complimented by everybody on the success of the day. The herd of Jersey cattle also won two prizes that September.

But the weather in both October and November had been dreadful and attendances – and their income - dropped like a stone. They needed to address the problem for this was likely to be the scenario every year. Bertie came up with the idea of building a large barn to house a new equestrian centre. This would be good because it could be used the whole year round. The proposal was put to the Council. The Councillors were in favour and immediately offered £75,000 towards the cost. There was, however, one proviso. This was that the funds would need to come from within that year's Council budget; in other words before the following April. This represented no problem as there was sufficient money to purchase the barn; the Council's contribution would be needed for the digging out of the foundations and erecting the structure.

Planning permission was required and application was made to the Council. The matter simply dragged on for month after month. Soon the Council's financial year end was fast approaching. Whatever the new owners said or did made no difference. By the time the necessary permission came through, it was too late and the funds were withheld.

A further application for financial assistance was submitted to come out of the Council's new financial year's budget but this was refused outright. This was a disaster because, as the Council knew only too well, the company could not survive without it. Why was the attitude now so very different from the original promises?

The cost of the barn itself had drained the partners of their remaining finance so what one earth could they do? They already had a bank overdraft and second mortgages on their homes to cover the original purchase price of the farm lease.

What happened then was even more of a puzzle. It transpired that the lease on the tennis courts on adjoining ground was due for renewal. Renewal of that lease was refused. What sense did that make?

Then followed the refusal to renew the lease of the indoor bowls club next to the tennis courts. What were the Council up to?

But the whole thing really came to a head when renewal of the lease on even more adjoining ground was refused. That particular leaseholder had his own miniature railway line. The perimeter was just over a quarter of a mile. Passengers could view the surrounding countryside and it was a great attraction for children seeing the steam engines in action. What was he to do? Where could he move his rail track, engines and carriages at such short notice? And at what cost? But 'go' the Council insisted.

Quite obviously the Council had other plans for the land - irrespective of the loss of convenience to others. It was adamant that no financial assistance would be made available to any of the parties concerned. They were on their own.

The farm, however, had its own lease with still another 13 years to run. The only way to evict the leaseholders would be for the Council to force them into liquidation or under a compulsory purchase order. The liquidation of the company with the lease would mean that it would automatically revert back to the freeholder. This was, of course, the easier option for the Council to exercise.

The lack of funding meant that the Company had no option but to file for liquidation with the loss of the £250,000 already invested in the business.

Several of the former leaseholders instructed solicitors to take action against the Council for breach of the Landlord and Tenants Act. This particular Act afforded protection to leaseholders from unscrupulous landlords. It also gave the right to renew a lease which was up for expiry unless the freeholder could show that he required the property for his own use.

The situation, however, soon became clear. The Government formally announced the final route of the new motorway. One of the proposed petrol stations and hotel would prove to be smack in the middle of the farm with lorry parking facilities covering the adjoining areas. From all of which the Council would profit substantially.

It then transpired that the Council had been aware of the likely route before disposing of the rare breeds' farm. They were aware also of the course open to them to recover the lease of it if required.

When the local press obtained the story, the Council claimed that it was only acting in the best interest of rate-payers. Which brings to mind a much used phrase: "Well, they would, wouldn't they!"

Fleet of Lorries

Reg and Colin were nice guys. Each was in his late thirties. Their employers manufactured tables and desks and the men had both worked at the factory for ten years. They were responsible for running the company's fleet of trucks which delivered the finished units all over the country. It was a good steady job and the only worry they ever faced was keeping a regular supply of drivers. They just seemed to come and go to where they could get the best rate of pay at any one time.

Out of the blue, one day Reg and Colin were summoned to the manager's office.

"Got some bad news, I'm afraid. The company has decided that it is going to contract out all deliveries. We have our hands full running our production lines without getting involved in maintaining vehicles and getting reliable drivers. Apart from that, we keep getting fluctuations in demand. Too many times we have both lorries and men standing idle. We can't afford that luxury any more."

Half-jokingly he added: "So, if you want to run your own business now is the time to do so. Just bid for the contract."

This was something of a shock to both of them. They were too taken aback to make any comment other than to ask if it was all definite. Was there a chance that the bosses might have a change of heart?

The answer was "Not a chance in Hell!"

They left feeling completely dumbstruck.

They had previously thought about starting out on their own but the huge initial cost involved in buying trucks put this out of the question.

"If we wanted to give it a go, perhaps the firm would do us a good deal on their existing trucks" suggested Colin. "They might be stuck with them otherwise."

After much thought and discussion they decided to ask their manager if the bosses would be prepared to consider selling them. If so, at what price.

"Well, if you are really serious, we would be glad to get rid of them. Apart from anything else we need the space. But you'll understand that, out of the six trucks, three of them are fairly new and are still subject to HP agreements. You have worked hard for us over the years and I feel we owe you something for that. I might be able to persuade the bosses to just let you take over the agreements on them. The older ones, I guess we could let you have for around £3,000 or £4,000 each. They might also be prepared to transfer to you what's left on the tax and insurance. I'll have a word this morning and see what I can do for you."

They were called back to the office an hour later.

"Well, it must be your lucky day for the bosses have agreed the suggestions I put to them. You can take over the agreements on the new lorries and the older ones you can have for £3,500 each. Do you want to go ahead?"

All of a sudden, things started to get exciting. These prices were much lower than they first envisaged. They reckoned that, on the rates being offered, they could easily afford the repayments on the loans. In fact they could, if necessary, replace one of the older trucks in the near future. They signed a contract accordingly.

Well, it all started off much better than they could have hoped. Even the drivers seemed keen for the project to succeed and a couple of them who had planned to leave stayed on. Strangely enough, they were almost as excited as Reg and Colin and agreed to wait until the end of the month for their wages.

Success followed success. But increased output from the factory forced the boys to replace one of the older lorries - at a cost of

£125,000 - sooner than expected. This put them deeper 'in the red' at the bank but they felt the potential additional income warranted the investment.

One morning, they were summoned to call to see the manager. Reg laughed and said: "I'm willing to bet that the rumour that they were going to take over another business is true and that they will need even more trucks."

"You'd better sit down" said the manager in a serious tone of voice. Reg and Colin did as they were bid.

"You are not going to like this much!" he continued. "You have probably heard the rumour that we are planning to expand. That is just rubbish. The reality is that we have been looking round for a buyer for our company for some time. Our machinery is now all out of date and we just haven't got sufficient capital to give the company a future. In reality, we had hoped that passing over the transport side of the business to you would have got us out of trouble. But it didn't. We have run out of money.

"The deal has now been signed and delivered. Our Company has been put into liquidation and the factory, machinery and staff have been taken over by a large group. This specialises in the sale of office equipment of all kinds on the net. Sadly for you, they have their own transport arrangements. So, sorry lads, but our contract with you in now terminated. We shall of course pay the outstanding accounts with you and pay for return trips on all trucks currently out on deliveries. I wish I could have made it easier for you but it is beyond my control. You will also need to find alternative accommodation for your trucks which must be off site in seven days."

"But what about the contract we have with you?" asked Colin.

"Well, that's just null and void. As I said, the Company who signed the contract is no longer in existence. Sorry."

There was a stony silence broken after two minutes by the manager who held out his hand and said once again "Sorry, lads."

Reg and Colin left the office without saying a word.

Once outside, Reg said "What the hell are we going to do now? Apart from anything else, where are we going to find sufficient space for the trucks which is secure?"

Both were worried sick at the thought of the debt hanging over their heads. If they were both to sell their houses, it still wouldn't be anything like sufficient. They would get little or nothing for the trucks as the market was at rick bottom.

"Well, they really did it to us this time Col! What on earth are we going to tell the girls?"

"Let's not panic but see if we can see a way out of this bl...y mess. We've got to tell the lads that they are all on a week's notice but that we'll try to find other contracts. If and when we do, we'll try to take them back on. Didn't Charlie say that he had a bit of land going spare? Do you think we could put the trucks down there?"

"Not a chance. His place is about as secure as the council's rubbish tip! What about Alf's place? He could take two and Bill might be able to take another. That leaves just four to find a home for - but two of those might be out on deliveries at any one time."

"That's if we get any orders. You do realise, of course, that we shall have to take up driving again ourselves, otherwise we shall have no income at all. I suppose we could each have one lorry outside our house."

"The girls won't like that! And there is that blessed weight limit for roadside parking at night. But I suppose we shall have to take a chance. We've no choice."

"One of us had better sort out storage for the lorries and the other get down to trying to find us some work."

"Right, let's do that. Have a word with the lads to see if they know of anywhere for the trucks and I'll do a bit of ringing around to see if there is anything going job-wise! You might also like to ask them to be on the look-out for jobs."

The drivers excelled themselves. One of them came back with the news that "Alf is able to help by taking three trucks in his yard. With his large German Shepherd on patrol at night, there is not much danger of their being vandalised."

Three others came back reporting that there were several firms they knew who could help them out as individuals by putting work their way but that they didn't want to get involved with a haulage contractor as such.

Colin said: "Well, why don't you accept the one lorry contracts as individuals? We'll lend you the trucks and you can pay us a hire charge by the day. We'll work out some figures so that you know what to charge your customers."

The lads liked this idea. All six of them came back with one vehicle contracts. They were much better off financially as 'owner-drivers' than they were just as drivers.

Reg and Colin were 'over the moon' because that got rid of the worry of getting contracts and parking facilities. Most of all, they didn't have to concern themselves with drivers leaving all the time.

In reality, this proved more profitable than actually operating a fleet of vehicles themselves. Their new style business just grew and grew on a self-drive hire basis. They no longer sought contracts for themselves but the list of drivers wanting to hire their lorries grew almost monthly. At the last count they had 33 vehicles out on hire and they were doing very nicely, thank you!

But how could they afford to keep buying vehicle costing £125,000 each? The simple answer was that they never did. Generally they bought second-hand ones at knock-down prices where the transport company concerned went into liquidation. There seemed to be an almost endless supply of those.

Right Man For The Job

Harry was a short stocky man of 53 years. He had spent a lot of his life working in the USA. He undertook a whole variety of occupations. When he finally decided that he preferred to live in England, he searched for something suitable by way of employment. The only trouble was that, although Harry had many talents, none of them carried the formal qualifications necessary to attract employers.

He was a positively charming man who really excelled himself at interviews on a man to man basis. He showed them that he had the power to make changes which would please both the management and staff alike. As he would say "I can change round your business 360 degrees." If the recipients had stopped and thought about the claim, they would have realised that this would have brought them back to where they were when they started. But Harry would keep them spellbound with such talk.

He regarded it as his right to apply for very senior positions when in reality he knew little or nothing about the work involved. He worked purely on the basis that there would always be somebody lower in rank than himself who could offer a solution to a problem. That same person would be able to provide him with ideas for advancement of the position. He was right, of course. His only problem was getting the interviews to start with.

When a leading estate agent in the area sought a senior negotiator to join the staff, Harry promptly offered his services. Instead of sending in his CV, he simply called at the address asking to see the owner. He would then apologise profusely for doing so without an appointment but would say "I thought you would like to see the person applying for such a responsible positon as opposed to reading his story."

Of course, in his usual way, Harry had little or no knowledge whatsoever of the estate business. He explained that things were done differently in the USA. He could soon adapt to his new circumstances. Harry got the job.

His boss was one of those people who had line after line of letters after their names. These were invariably from a variety of trade associations where the payment of a small annual fee warranted an associateship membership for display to all.

Harry had nothing, of course. Nothing, that is, apart from the letters 'LTSanF' after his name. This qualification suddenly appeared for the first time on the production of his new visiting card. When questioned, even by his new employer, he said that he hoped he could be forgiven for not wishing to discuss the qualification as this represented to him something rather distressing incident in his life. Perhaps he would be allowed to explain this later when the bitterness behind it all had subsided.

His friends tried hard to work out the qualification by coming up with such things as "Licentiate Trader in Sanitary Fittings". Harry would neither confirm nor deny this as it was: "All too personal".

With the help of his underlings, Harry succeeded in the job for some five years before he grew tired of the work and sought another challenge. That was Harry to a tee; five years in one job was more than sufficient.

His next application for employment was for the position of Assistant Head of Operations for a vehicle parts company in the Midlands.

Harry explained that "As I had occasion to drive the 159 miles up here on an unexpected business trip, I thought I would kill two birds with one stone by calling to see if it were a convenient moment for a brief chat about the position on offer with your Head of Personnel."

The job was his when the 'LTSanF' qualification mysteriously disappeared from his card only to be replaced by 'FTBA'.

As he had left the estate business, he finally agreed to explain that 'LTSanF' stood for: 'Last Train to San Fernando'. But promptly refused to explain the 'FTBA' as it was "all too personal." His friends are now endeavouring to find the meaning behind 'FTBA'!

Could it have been 'First Train Back Again'? Nobody knew. They would have to wait until Harry changed his job again in another five years.

Rules of Golf

Nobody had actually explained to 6 year old Matthew about the courtesies usually observed when watching golf. But his father was a most keen golfer and Matthew had accompanied him to many professional tournaments.

It came as second nature for him to remain quiet and perfectly still while a player was addressing the ball. He realised also that it was polite to applaud loudly once the ball was struck.

Whilst walking with his grandparents along a footpath close to the local gold club, Matthew came to a complete halt on seeing a player very close to him at the tee about to play a stroke. His grandparents were really impressed that one so young should be aware of the finer points of the game. Their admiration soon turned to complete embarrassment when the lad burst into instant applause once the ball had been struck.

A furious golfer turned immediately to see who had had the nerve to poke fun at his sliced shot which had soared like a bird only to land in the trees about ten yards to the left of the tee.

The grandparents didn't know where to look but their relief was immediate when, on seeing the lad still applauding loudly, both the golfer and his partner burst out laughing. All ended well.

Keeping It In The Family

"Hello Bertie." said Alan. "Nice to see you again" he continued "and at what an opportune moment. I was just wondering whether you could give one of my friends a bit of a helping hand. He hasn't got much money – in fact, he hasn't got any money at all – but he has this terrible depression. I said that you were the best psychotherapist around and would be the very chap to sort him out."

Bertie thought for a minute before replying: "Well, Alan, it was kind of you to think of me but I seem to have acquired quite a few extra clients of late. I doubt really whether I can take on more in the foreseeable future. I just haven't got room in my diary – irrespective as to whether the client has any money. But, as it is you, if it is a fairly straight-forward case to handle, I'll see if I can slide him in for a brief session."

"It stems from the fact that Tony is bi-sexual. He loves his wife and kids but there is Ian. He has a fling with him every so often."

"That seems pretty straight-forward, said Bertie. It sounds to me like a case of guilt complex but I don't like to pre-judge issues."

"I just wish it were that simple. Perhaps I should add that Tony's wife, Betty, is also bi-sexual. She has the odd wandering off the straight and narrow with Tony's cousin Peter and also Peter's wife, Jane. Jane, incidentally, is a lesbian.

"I must confess it has been pointed out that my wife, Judy, has been seen in her company from time to time. I haven't pressed the subject with Judy but I have had my suspicions on her sexuality for some time.

I guess that would finish up with discussions over my own. You have probably guessed from our days at college that my preference can be mixed at times and I have been seeing Ian's brother Lenny on and off for quite a few years. Nothing too serious you understand for I don't want to lose Judy - or her sister, Mary, come to that. Mary's a good sort. Always up for a quickie when Judy is out walking the dog. As it happens, Mary is a bit of a cracker when she's in the mood for men – which isn't that often! Perhaps I should just add also that Mary is Lenny's sister-in-law and Tony's cousin by marriage."

"I said 'in a few words', Alan. I hope you aren't expecting me to remember all those names. Sometimes I have a job to remember my own! It does all sound very complicated and I don't know whether I really have either the time or energy to even start to sort out that lot!"

Alan responded "It would mean a lot to me, Bertie, if for old time's sake you could just slip Tony in for five minutes of your time. Forget the background information – that's not important."

Bertie's diary was maintained by his receptionist but, when he has an appointment away from his office, he always too the diary with him in his briefcase. That way he could record any new appointment with the client he was visiting.

He turned the pages slowly desperately looking for a gap. His eyes opened wide when he reached Wednesday, for, on that day each week, he always tried to keep at least the afternoon free for emergencies. It really was full to the brim with just a little slot late in the afternoon.

He looked at Harry and said: "If it really is that urgent, I see from my diary that I do have a single slot next Wednesday late afternoon. If you remember, you have an appointment with me, yourself, at 4 o'clock that day. At a push, I could see Tony at 5.0 pm - but for a very short time. I suggest most strongly that you don't tell him about your appointment as that might confuse things more than a little."

Of course, what Bertie failed to appreciate at the time was the actual number of new patients his receptionist had lined up for that Wednesday.

It was going to come as a great surprise to him to find that it was Tony's wife, Betty, who was booked in for 9.0 am; followed by Tony's cousin, Peter, at 10.0; his wife, Jane at 11.0; Judy at 12 noon; Lenny's brother at 2.0pm and Mary at 3.0 pm before Alan arrived at 4.0 pm followed by Tony at 5.0 pm.

But what was going to come as an even greater surprise was when Mary arrived at 3 o'clock complete with her dog and suggested that Bertie's receptionist took the dog for a walk!

Pay-Back Time

THEY had no spirits, wine, fancy goods, cigarettes or souvenirs – just the extra box of 50 cigars over the permitted allowance. Paul had bought these at Dallas airport as a last minute thought.

Having been warned on the plane that the Customs at Stanstead airport were particularly tough, Paul and Mary went through the Goods to Declare area. They felt rather isolated as they were the only people on the flight from America who went through that section.

There was just one officer on duty who, looking up in a rather disinterested way, enquired: "And just what have you got to declare, sir?"

Paul explained that they hadn't got any alcohol, perfume, gifts, cigarettes or other items on which duty might be payable and was about to continue when he was interrupted by a somewhat bored voice: "Very good, sir, but what exactly brought you through this section?"

"A box of 50 cigars over the limit – which were given to me by a dear friend as a parting gift at the airport. I couldn't really refuse to take it could I!" Paul replied.

"Well, that will be £24.80 in duty, sir!"

Forgetting that they were supposed to have been a gift, Paul said crossly: "Well, you can keep them then because they only cost me £12!"

"Ah, in that case, sir, I'll only charge you just £10 in duty."

Paul was furious that he should be victimised in this way but reluctantly paid the £10.

He swore a solemn oath to get his own back and, on each annual trip to the USA, Paul brought back with him an extra 50 cigars over the limit without declaring them.

This worked without a hitch until Paul gave up smoking. He still brought back the cigars as a matter of principle. He could justify this because he had several friends who still smoked cigars and he gave them away as gifts.

Sadly for Paul, one by one, all his friends bar one followed his good example. What on earth would he do with the positive mountain of cigars in the cupboard if his friend were to stop smoking as well?

There was a principle involved here which had to be maintained. He had to find something else to replace the cigars. His first thought was to switch to bottles of whisky but the size and weight of the bottles would create more problems than enough.

Lucky for Paul, his wife came up with a sensible solution.

"Why don't you simply buy a very small but expensive bottle of perfume? You could get that in your vest pocket!" The problem was solved. Quite a clever girl that one!

Tit for Tat?

Sean's son, Paul, who was 13 years of age at the time, had been knocked over on a zebra crossing by a 'hit-and-run' car driver. He had laid in a coma for several weeks with multiple fractures and head injuries. But Paul recovered and, although still walking with a limp, he managed to get out and about on his own. Luckily, his brain was not damaged.

One late afternoon, he came home in a bit of a state because he said he had seen the very car that had knocked him over and he had got the registration number. Sean immediately went with Paul to the local police station to report what had been seen. The police were most helpful and said that they would trace the vehicle immediately. They would be back in touch when they had some news.

Well, they came back as promised but their news was not what Sean or his son wanted to hear. It was obvious that the owner of the car who, according to the police could only be described as a 22 year old yob, was the guilty party all right. The problem was that the vehicle had had any damage repaired and been completely re-painted privately. It could not be pinpointed as being the vehicle in question. At the same time, the driver had an airtight alibi provided by two of his friends.

Sean and Paul were very angry but appreciated that the police were powerless to take the matter further. They had to admit that Paul might just have made a mistake on the make of car because it was all over in a flash. He had heard the engine and turned round in time just to see the vehicle a few yards away. Then, being in a coma for such a long time, placed a question mark over the whole thing.

Sean enjoyed a game of darts and played for his team at the local pub most Friday evenings. They were in one of the top leagues which meant that most games were televised. He was playing a match one evening when he overheard a quiet conversation between three young men in the opposing team who were waiting to play; one stood adjacent to the dartboard.

"Did you ever hear any more from the police about that kid you knocked over?" one of them asked.

"No, they couldn't prove a thing. There was doubt whether he got the right car and you two providing the alibi was sufficient for them to close the book on the case, thank Heavens! I was sorry about it but I wasn't prepared to put my career at risk as a footballer. As you know, I've got a major trial tomorrow for Bedford Albion FC. I've only got this one last chance to make it big time - so I've even got to go easy on the booze tonight. Don't let me drink too much."

The person speaking was the one next to the dartboard and he matched to a tee how the police had described him: a 22 year old yob. Sean looked at the match card and saw that his name was Hank.

It was Sean's turn to play next. He was a very tall man with arms to match so that it seemed at times as though they almost reached the dartboard. There was absolute silence as Sean checked the score and decided that his side needed a three followed by a double top for that game.

He took careful aim at the board but, as his arm came forward to release the dart, he appeared to trip on the marker mat. The dart left his hand at a tremendous rate and went straight through Hank's shoe and foot which almost impaled him to the floor. As Hank fell backwards he grabbed out at the nearest thing to break his fall which was the main, very heavy TV camera and metal framework. This fell on top of him, badly gashing his knee and thigh. But Sean was falling forward too and, as he collided with the dartboard, it fell off the wall landing on Hank's head. Blood spurted out everywhere and the guy was in absolute agony.

"I'm so terribly sorry" said Sean "but my foot slipped. I hope you're OK."

"OK? You lunatic! Just look at what you have done. For goodness sake, somebody ring for an ambulance and get me to hospital."

The paramedic arrived within five minutes. He said that Hank would be all right but that he needed half a dozen stitches in his head, four or more in his thigh and that his tibia was quite obviously fractured. The chances were, too, that the bone in his foot was badly chipped. He added that it would probably mean at least two or three weeks in hospital and walking could well prove to be a problem for a couple of months or more.

The darts match was abandoned. On his way home, Sean reflected on the events of the evening. He remembered that they all had had to sign an entry form when applying for inclusion in the league. This stated that people participating in the competition did so entirely at their own risk. A player could not be held responsible for any injury to another player or damage to his possessions.

When he got home, Sean explained what had happened to Paul and to the rest of his family. Understandably, they were all most upset at the very thought that Hank would be out of action for the foreseeable future. The fact that his professional football playing was now a thing of the past was truly regrettable! Their grief was such that they found it necessary to drown their sorrows in a second bottle of champagne.

"Cheers and a speedy return to good health, Hank!"

Right Change

One afternoon, Bill called to see his mother, Maud, who was 85 years of age and a widow.

He simply could not believe his ears when she confided in him that, after no less than 65 years of support of the Labour Party, she had decided to join the local Conservatives.

He really could not believe that his Mother, a 'cockney' by birth - because she was born at Poplar within the sounds of Bow Bells – had changed sides.

Bill asked her what finally persuaded her to make the change.

The answer was easy. For some years, she had gone on the Labour Party's coach regularly for a day's outing to the Kent countryside. This had involved her getting a bus down to the town centre from where the coach left.

She had been informed by her neighbour that the Conservative coach outings started from a different location. This was just two hundred yards up the road from where she lived. As this did not involve a bus journey she had joined the Conservative Party!

There really was no answer to her logic but Harry was quick to add: "You may be a member of the Conservative Party but you don't have to vote for them at an election!"

Fishy Tale

Stan had four friends who were equally as passionate as he about sea fishing. Once a month they would drive down in one car to Deal and hire a boat for the day. The boat would be booked in advance along with the bait so that there would be no delay on arrival. They would always take with them some frozen herring. This was just in case the fishing was good and they ran out of lugworms. The boat they took each time was called, rather appropriately, 'Seaweed'.

It was a good sea boat but, with the strong tides which run along the coast in that part of the world, five people in the boat were enough. Fishing lines all ran in one direction and more than five rods would often mean that lines could get terribly tangled.

They used Stan's car as his was the only one which could seat five people and carry all the fishing tackle in the boot. Plus, of course, they needed room for the huge catch of fish they optimistically hoped to have.

The first person for Stan to collect was Ted at 6 o'clock in the morning. Next it was George at five minutes past six, followed by Bob a couple of minutes later and, lastly, Jim at 6.15 am.

Stan pulled up outside Ted's house. His front door was always already open and Ted came out closing the door behind him. He threw his gear in the boot and climbed in the front seat next to Stan. It was virtually the same with both George, and Bob; they were always awaiting the sound of the car and by 6.15 am they would all arrive outside Jim's house.

Bob usually had the job of getting out of the back seat to tap gently on Jim's door. He was never quite ready. The door would open after two or three minutes. The five were ready to go on the two hour trip to Deal.

There was not a lot of room in the car because of the heavy clothing they wore against the cold in the winter months. There was little or no shelter from the wind on the boat but it was cosy in the car with the heater going. Almost invariably a couple of the passengers in the back would fall asleep on the way.

One particular Sunday, the usual four were already in the car. It pulled up outside Jim's house. Bob got out of the car and tapped on the door. No reaction. Bob rang the door-bell and, after a few seconds, the light went on in the bedroom. The window opened and Jim was in his pyjamas. "I'm just coming now" said Jim "I won't be a few seconds." Five minutes later, the front door opened and there was Jim still pulling up his trousers over the top of his pyjamas. "I'm coming, don't worry!"

Bob had got back into the car leaving room for Jim to squeeze in last. As he did, Jim said "Sorry about that, my alarm didn't go off."

In reality this was Jim to a tee. Always a good reason why he wasn't where he should be. But he was nice bloke and a useful chap to have around for free advice as he was a Certified Accountant. "Otherwise quite a nice bloke" George would always joke.

So they set off for Deal and arrived just after 8.15 am. They always went early in case of breakdown but also to enjoy a hearty full English breakfast before they went out in the boat. George always seemed to tuck in more than most with an extra couple of slices of toast with his bacon and eggs "So that I have something to bring up when I am sick" he would say.

George would never miss a trip but he was a terrible sailor and was always sick on the boat. It was probably the roughness of the sea coupled with the long car ride which did it.

The fishing that day was absolutely brilliant. Stan caught a cod which was all of 25 lbs and Bob managed a plaice of around 4 lbs. But everybody caught fish and they went home very happy bunnies.

About a week later, Bob met Stan in the High Street when he said that the smell in his car was really dreadful. He had looked everywhere but he could find nothing. He thought that they might have left a fish or two in the boot but nothing was found.

Another week passed and Gary rang Bob to tell him that he could barely get into his car now because of the smell but another search had still found nothing. After another week, Gary could couldn't use his car at all. He had taken it to the garage to see if something was caught up underneath. Nothing was discovered there. It looked as though somebody else would have to provide the transport for the next fishing trip.

However, the garage did eventually unscrew and take out the rear seats. There they found the unfrozen herring in a newspaper that had fallen out of Jim's pocket when he climbed into the car on the last trip. Sitting on the fish jammed it right down between the back of the seat and the cushion. Of course, he knew the unwritten rule that all fish had to go in the boot of the car along with all fishing tackle but Jim was still half-asleep that day and forgot all about it.

The mystery was solved. Jim wasn't very popular with Stan for some time but, from then on, he was always standing at the front door waiting for the car to arrive with his frozen fish in one hand and his fishing tackle in the other ready to be put in the boot.

Live & Learn

Rob and Mary were looking forward to their holiday in the north of Cyprus. They had visited the south of the island previously and had enjoyed it so much that they wanted to visit the area in the north. It was just two years after the invasion of the north by Turkish troops. Most of the Greek Cypriots had been driven to the south of the island.

They had a friend living in the UK, Mustafa Ratip. He was a Turkish Cypriot by birth and he gave them advice as to where to go, what to see and where to stay. In fact, he even got his brother Ahmed, who was still living in Cyprus, to make contact with them on their arrival to welcome them and show them the sights.

The outward journey was long because of the compulsory stop-over at Istanbul. Their excitement on arrival at the new airport in the north was greatly diminished when, stepping down from the plane, they were confronted by heavily armed Turkish military personnel. There were welcoming smiles all round, so the incident was soon forgotten.

As Rob and Mary were taken by car to their hotel, they were amazed at the lack of traffic on the road. They did not see another car on the five mile journey and the only people to be seen were sentries on duty every quarter of a mile along the roadside. On passing the second, Rob just raised his hand in a gesture of friendship when the sentry came smartly to attention and saluted him. Ron told Mary that the soldiers obviously recognised him to be a person of high rank. The only comment she made was that the troops were probably bored silly and just saluted for something to do. This hand-waving became a regular feature of the holiday when Rob and Mary decided to hire a car to travel around. They were saluted wherever they went and were later informed that the troops saluted everybody to try to make visitors feel welcome and not be afraid of the military

Their hotel just outside Kyrenia (or 'Girne' as it is now called) was absolutely first class. It had its own beach. The dining room was actually built out into the sea.

Ahmed was waiting for them at the hotel when they arrived and his first task was to buy them a welcoming drink. They all enjoyed a large gin and tonic. In fact, it was just about the best they had ever tasted. They arranged to meet him again the following day close to the harbour.

As it happens, they arrived earlier than Ahmed and Rob went to the bar to buy a gin and tonic for them both.

"I'm very sorry, sir" said the bartender "But the sale of alcohol is not permitted on Ataturk Day in Turkey or, indeed, in any of its possessions." Well, that was something of a blow as they were looking forward to their drink. Most reluctantly they accepted a replacement orange juice which, in all fairness, was delicious – but not quite the same as a 'G & T'.

Shortly afterwards, Ahmed arrived. "You don't want to drink that stuff; let me get you a gin and tonic." Rob smiled and said: "Thanks, Ahmed, but I think you may have forgotten something, haven't you?"

"Forgotten something?" queried Ahmed.

Rob, with a knowing look replied: "It's Ataturk Day and the sale of alcoholic refreshment is not allowed."

"Oh dear. That's a pity" came the reply "but we really must stick to the rules."

With that Ahmed went up to the bar and ordered "Three Seven-Up specials, please." And passed a gin and tonic to both Rob and Mary.

"It looks like we are going to have a great holiday here, Mary!" said Rob taking a second large sip from his glass. "We'll just have to learn a slightly different language!"

Some Bargains Are Better Than Others

Harry and Peggy were a perfect match. Each had an eye for a bargain. They had a lovely group of very patient friends, all with different interests. On every visit to whatever house rotation dictated, there was always a long, blow by blow tale of the latest acquisition by Harry and Peggy for their home, car, caravan or holiday.

The dinner engagement one evening last March was typical in that Harry had heard of this special Caribbean cruise. Not only was it at "The lowest price known to man" as Harry put it, but all the booze was free. "Champagne for breakfast, wine with lunch and dinner followed by aperitifs by the gallon. Free beer and spirits were available all day between meals – all at no extra cost. What a bargain!" he said.

The itinerary did indeed look good and included business class seats on the plane flying out of Heathrow – and even a free taxi to take them to the airport.

What was the catch? Well, there appeared not to be one. It was all *bona fide* and the holiday carried the usual ABTA guarantee.

Harry suggested that they made up a party but Tom and Mary were already committed to visit their grandchildren in Cornwall at that time and the other two, Freda and Reg, had similar conflicting arrangements. So it was not to be.

Discussions on the future trip were a regular feature of meetings. Harry would produce maps and charts to show the others exactly where they were going to be on any one particular day. In fact, it was quite a relief when the departure date approached for that would be a little respite from the trip. That was, of course, until Harry and Peggy came home. They all knew full well what the topic of conversation would be for the following month at least! But they were all good friends and enjoyed Harry and Peggy's company.

About a week into the trip, Tom received a telephone call from Peggy. It was a very bad line and Peggy was greatly distressed. It was difficult to fully understand was she was saying. At first he thought that Peggy said that Tom had food poisoning and kept asking how Harry was doing. Was he in hospital?

You can just imagine how Tom felt when Peggy stopped him short and shouted down the line: "Harry has been eaten by an alligator!" With that the line went dead and, as he didn't know where Peggy was or even the name of the travel company, he was unable to return the call. He just had to wait for her to call again.

"Who was that on the phone, dear?" asked Mary. When Tom told her what had happened, she screamed at him that he was an absolute fool and had got it all wrong. She just couldn't believe what she had heard.

As a result, they had to wait patiently for further news but Tom told Reg what he thought he had heard. "It can't be!" joked Reg. "I can't imagine any alligator wanting to eat Harry – he would be too tough an old bird for even the biggest of them". Even Tom was beginning to doubt what he had heard and remained silent on the matter.

Ten days passed. There was still no further calls from Peggy. Suddenly, out of the blue, a car pulled up outside and out stepped Peggy. Tom immediately called Mary who rushed to the front door to greet her.

After a short embrace, they went inside and sat down in silence in the sitting room where they were joined by Tom.

"So you've heard the news" said Peggy. "Well, not really" said Mary. "I'm afraid that the line went dead before Tom got the message. What exactly has happened? Is Harry all right?"

"All right? How can he be all right when he been eaten by an alligator?"

"When Tom told me about the incident, we thought he had got it wrong. Oh dear, what on earth can we say or do?"

"Well, you can't really say or do anything! What has happened has happened and we'll just have to live with it."

Tom chipped in "Haven't you got a claim on the travel company?"

"Well, in all fairness, not really dear. It was partly Harry's own fault. In fact it was all his own stupid fault!"

"How did it happen then? Would it be too painful for you to tell us?"

"Well, it's OK now" responded Peggy. "I'm getting used to the idea. You see, the ship called in at Miami and we joined a party to go to the Everglades. This included a ride on a swamp glider and a visit by boat to a village of the Miccosukee tribe of Indians. It was the usual type of rubbish that you get at these places. We were invited to sample what can only be described as their local hooch and rice bread. The local brew was very strong. Harry had already had half a bottle of champagne with his breakfast and a few beers before he left the ship, so the hooch tasted quite good. It was free so Harry had three or four glasses. But the rice bread was inedible. Not wishing to offend anybody, Harry stuffed this in his pocket when nobody was looking.

"We then returned to this small boat which was to take us back across this long stretch of swamp water to re-join the coach. We got halfway across when the engine packed up. The guy in charge radioed through to the tour organiser who said that another boat would be with us shortly to tow us back to land; so we just had to wait.

"With nothing else to do, Harry took the rice bread from his pocket and, with his hand splashing in the water to attract the fish, tried to get them to take the bread from his hand. He was quite successful in this until there was a large splash. The fish disappeared only to be replaced by this four feet long alligator. This took not only the bread but Harry's hand as well. He was being pulled into the water by the alligator while four of five of the other passengers were holding onto Harry for dear life. They were determined not to let him go. The boatman picked up the heavy anchor and brought it down on the alligator's head. This caused the teeth to bite completely through Harry's wrist and the alligator made off with Harry's hand still in its mouth.

"As luck would have it, we had the ship's doctor in our party and he quickly applied a tourniquet to stop the profuse bleeding. He used his mobile phone to ring for a helicopter to take Harry to the nearest hospital, which was about 25 miles away. He was in there for a week but was allowed to fly home with me yesterday. He's out there in the car now and has asked to be forgiven for not coming in but he is feeling pretty sorry for himself and doesn't want anybody to see him in such a state.

"But I am sure he will soon be able to tell you all about it in much more detail when we are scheduled to meet up in a couple of weeks' time."

Harry 'dined out' on his experience for month after month after month when the length of the alligator grew rapidly and the exploits more daring by the telling. There were occasions when several rather wished that the alligator had taken all of Harry and not just his hand.

The Evacuee

Ten-year-old Bobby Johnson was the youngest of three children in his family. He was always treated as a baby by his two elder sisters, Betty aged 17 and Hilda who was 15.

The family lived at Erith within half a mile of the River Thames in North West Kent.

The Thames represented a map for German bombers to approach London in WW2. There was much industry on both sides of the river so this, too, represented a useful target.

It was not long before a bomb landed just 50 yards from their home, causing broken windows and tiles blown off the roof. This resulted in all but the father being evacuated to a village close to Folkestone in Kent called Peene. Bobby's father worked in a munitions factory and could not leave home.

Peene was a lovely little village with a farm in the middle of it. Unfortunately, it was just a mile or so from the RAF fighter-pilot station at Hawkinge - which also presented a useful target for the enemy. After just two weeks, it was realised that the evacuation was '*from the frying pan into the fire*'. They were moved back to their home.

But just one month later, those children still at school – of which Bobby was one – were offered evacuation to Yorkshire. Bobby's family agreed that he should go with several other local children. Their destination proved to be a woollen mill town called Elland. This was in Yorkshire situated roughly halfway between Huddersfield and Halifax.

Some of the evacuees were a bit unfortunate in that the host family regarded them as slaves to undertake any work around the house that was required. Others were harshly treated and it was rumoured that several were sexually abused.

Bobby, on the other hand, stayed with a really lovely middle-aged lady called Edith Marsden. Her husband was a corporal serving his country in the army medical corps. He was based in Conway, North Wales which, in all fairness, was not exactly the centre of warfare.

'Aunty Edith', as she became known, was an extremely kind person. She had a lovely voice and sang contralto in the local Baptist Church choir at Blackley just out of the town itself. She took Bobby along with her. He came across as a 'natural' when it came to singing and, with his parents' prior approval, finished up having his voice trained. He was taken occasionally to hear the famous Huddersfield Choral Society.

Notwithstanding his secret longing to be back with his family in Kent, he enjoyed life in Elland. He joined several of the local lads in fishing for goldfish in the woollen mill lake. The goldfish were placed there to reduce the weed which could clog the machinery when water was drawn in to dampen the wool. As the fish bred, there were too many in the lake. The mill owners closed their eyes to the lads fishing for them. They used literally 'bent pins' as traditional hooks could harm the mouths of the fish.

It caused momentary panic when young Bobby wrote home saying that he would be spending his first three months at Elland in prison. He said that the prison surroundings had a dismal feel to them. They were dark and shabby. Although the doors were never closed, there was always a claustrophobic air about the place. He could see the school housing other children through the barred windows.

The panic ceased immediately when he went on to explain that, after three months, the school would be able to accommodate all the evacuees. They would then be moved from the 17th Century prison museum where they were being taught as one class.

The evacuees found it advantageous to learn to speak with a Yorkshire accent quite quickly. After a comparatively short time, it was difficult to tell the evacuees from the local children. However, the local children did seem more advanced educationally. This was probably because they had not had their education interrupted as much as the evacuees. Schooling in Kent during the war was always being interrupted by sirens going every hour or so and the children having to run to the school shelters. It was not really surprising that all but one of the evacuees failed their 11+ exam. Bobby was not the lucky one.

When the war was over, Bobby returned to his home. And, shortly afterwards, he was called for a voice test at Southwark Cathedral. He was accepted as a chorister but this would be subject to his sitting and passing the entrance examination to St. Olaves Grammar School. This particular school, which was some 500 years old, was situated close to the Cathedral on the south bank of the Thames opposite the Tower of London. It acted as a choir school to enable choristers to attend services during school hours as required. Bobby passed the entrance examination and spent four happy years at the Cathedral.

Bobby kept in touch with the 'Auntie Edith' for many years and she visited him and his wife at their home in Kent. Years later, he took his wife to Elland and was able to show her the town and the actual house to which he had been evacuated. They found the house without difficulty but, alas, the Blackley Baptist Church - which was on the top of the hill away from the town – had been incorporated into the M62 motorway.

Quite recently, Bobby met a man on business who went by the name of Michael Bennett. In casual conversation, Bobby asked Michael where he lived. The answer came: "It's no use my giving you the name of my town. Nobody's ever heard of it. It's a little place in Yorkshire – halfway between 'uddersfield and 'alifax."

Bobby said: "That sounds very much like Elland to me!"

"How the devil did you know that?" Michael asked.

"Well, it's a long story but I was evacuated there during the war. I lived at 70 Catherine Street with Edith Marsden."

"I know the very house and I knew the Marsden family well. Lovely people. I was their insurance agent for many years. Small world, isn't it!"

Greener Grass

You always knew when Alec Jeavons was in the pub. His lectures were non-stop on what was wrong with the country, the Government, the bosses and the over-paid employees in certain industries.

"Just explain to me here and now why the workers at Fords earn on average twice as much as we do in this factory. It's just not right and we need to get the Government to bring out a law to stop this kind of thing – otherwise the country will go to the dogs even faster than it is at the moment."

But the Ford workers were not the only ones in the line of fire. "What about all those lazy blokes working down the mines. They get even more than the Ford workers and most of them only went down the mines to start with to avoid being called up for the army.

"Did you know they take home more than three times what we get paid. And just look at those laziest of all blokes who call themselves Dockers. Dockers? They only work one day a week and they get nearly as much as the miners. Also, that pay is supplemented by the stuff they nick off the boats they're unloading!"

In actuality, it was everybody's fault other than Alec's. He was the only person in the country who put in a full day's work for a pittance. Well, perhaps a 'full day' might be a slight exaggeration as he was the union representative. He was allowed time off to devote to union business. More often than not, he only did three hours a day on his factory lathe. And most of those three hours were spent in discussion with his workmates about lack of Health and Safety in the factory.

One evening at the pub, Charlie Jackson pointed out the advert in the local paper about workers required at Fords. They needed more men to work on the new extended assembly line.

Without saying anything to the others, Alec applied for a job there and managed to get it. His so-called principles went out of the window at the thought of getting the extra money. Of course, he omitted to tell the new bosses that he was a union man. But that could come later once he had his feet under the table and had showed the others how the assembly line job should be done.

Alec's old bosses were heart-broken, of course, at the news that Alec was leaving. It must have been a pure coincidence that flags were on display on the day of his departure!

After his first day in his new job, Alec was noticeably absent from the pub. Probably the first night he had missed in over five years. It was very peaceful and there was not the usual buzz of conversation.

The second night came and there was still no Alec. After his absence for a third night, Charlie decided he would pop in on Alec on the way home to see if all was well. Alec's wife came to the door. "You'd better come in, Charlie, and see for yourself what that job has done to him!"

There was Alec sprawled on the settee barely able to move. He ached from head to foot.

"What's the matter Alec?"

"The matter?" replied Alec. It's that bloody job at Fords that's done for me. I knew I would be in trouble the very first day. They started to spray the car and I was still trying to get the second wheel on the damn thing. They warned me then that my performance would have to improve otherwise the new owner of a car would finish up driving along the road and I would be running along-side fitting the last component. I have tried very hard to keep up but I can't see that I could possibly survive there. Believe me, those blokes deserve every last penny they get! I was wondering whether my old job was still going. Have they filled it yet?"

"Well, yes, they have actually."

"A young bloke I expect full of the old energy I always had!"

"Well, no, not really, Alec. They got this OAP who needed a part-time job and he comes in for a couple of hours just two mornings a week."

Charlie then added: "I feel a bit bad about that new job of yours because I had heard before that you really needed to be young and fit to work on the assembly line. But, of course, you didn't tell us you were going to try for it. In any case, you really needed to find out for yourself because you wouldn't trust what I said.

Charlie continued: "In fact, I can tell you now that, some time ago, I saw a job advertised for working down the mines. I went for an interview and was offered the job subject to my first going down to the coal face to see if I could work in the conditions which prevailed. Some people experience claustrophobia and can't work in a mine.

"Well, we got into this lift cage and it dropped like a stone. I thought the cable had broken or something but the guy in charge said that was normal and everything was OK. He said it was a quarter of a mile down but it felt more like we were going to the centre of the earth. I was not happy. In fact, I was scared stiff!

"But the journey down was only the start of the problems for me. When we got to the level, we walked for ages to the coal face itself dodging the little trucks full of coal which came round the bends at an alarming rate with little or no warning.

"Then came the big blow. To get to the actual coal face involved crawling along this four feet high tunnel which was about six feet wide. Mind you, it was only ten feet long but it felt more like going under the Alps.

"The terrifying thing for me was when the bloke working there said 'mind your feet'. About six inches from where I stood, what I can only described as a chain saw with hooks sticking out from it sprang into action. The chain itself ran from the machine cutting into the coal face and back to the machine bringing with it bits of coal in the hooks.

"I can tell you now, that I couldn't get out of that place fast enough and I swore that never again would I ever set foot in a mine. Needless to say, I told them exactly what they could do with their job and the extra money that went with it."

The following night Alec was back in the pub with his mates but it was only the Dockers that were mentioned as not earning their pay! The Ford workers and the miners miraculously escaped criticism.

All At Sea

"Surely there must be a more practical way than this?" asked Bob of the Cunard Booking Office.

"No, that really is the best way." came the reply.

"So you have this special offer of flying from the UK to New York and returning on board the 'QE2' ship and vice versa. And rather than issue me with a return cruise ticket, I buy two special offers for each of us and throw away the airline tickets?"

"Yes, that's absolutely right. I'm sorry, sir, but you are saving £2,000 by doing this and you asked me for the best way to do it. In addition, of course, you get two days in Manhattan with the accommodation paid."

"Well, it is much cheaper than what we have paid before so, OK then, I'll have two for me and two for my wife but I have never heard of anything so daft in all my life! Have you dear?" he said, turning to his wife, Maisie.

The cruise out to New York was great but, as was almost invariably the case, the ship ran into a couple of days of fog halfway across. That was where the cold Icelandic current met the warm Golf Stream. Bob and Maisie just accepted that because it was nature at work.

But what was always a bit disconcerting was when the Captain announced on each trip over the tannoy that: "I thought you might like to know that we are now just ten miles away from where the Titanic sank. But, of course, this is a modern ship and that just can't happen to us." Somehow that phrase seemed to ring a bell.

THE SQUATTERS & OTHERS

The crossing took just five days and the ship arrived at 6 o'clock on the Saturday morning. Then followed the short-ish flight down to Charlotte, North Carolina. This was where Bob and Maisie's son and grandchildren lived. They stayed with their son for four weeks and then flew up to New York for the cruise home.

It was not worth changing out of the summer clothes for the short flight back to New York. They could change once on board the ship. Bob was in shorts with his beach shirt on display. Maisie was dressed similarly. The only thing they carried as hand luggage was Maisie's bag and Bob's shoulder bag which contained their money, passports and tickets. There was one other thing and that was a huge quilt they had purchased which was too large to go into any of their cases. It was easier to just carry it.

The plan was that they would land with enough time before the cruise for a quick look out to sea from Battery Point to Staten Island before boarding the ship. But their arrival by plane was the start of the problem. Their luggage missed the flight and was still in Charlotte.

"Don't worry at all sir, we'll have it sent up on the next flight in an hour's time."

"Well, we had better wait here for it to arrive."

"That won't be necessary, sir. This happens quite frequently and we'll have it sent directly to the ship for you. You can rely on us."

Bob and Maisie boarded the ship. They waited and waited but departure time was fast approaching and there was still no sign of their luggage. They told the ship's chief steward but he said: "We have this on every trip, sir. Just stop worrying and leave it to us! In fact, your luggage may already be on board but we shall no way of knowing for a couple of hours."

The ship sailed but the luggage was still in Charlotte.

The ship supplied a few basic things like toothbrushes and soap but it was necessary to buy everything else. Bob and Maisie were told that the shops on board would open after dinner and were given a voucher for £200 'to help out'.

They went into dinner and there were glares all round! Beach clothes in the dining room indeed!!! They were seated at a table next to the CEO of Shell International, Jason Matthews and his wife, Marie. After the immediate shock of seeing how they were dressed, they both proved to be most sympathetic after hearing the tale of woe. This helped make life a little more bearable for Bob and Maisie but the glares continued from other passengers.

After dinner, the shops had none of the major items required. It was a case of' make do and mend'. Maisie bought a long Minnie-mouse tee-shirt which would have to act as a nightdress. She bought also an 'afternoon' dress. Bob purchased the only trousers available which were track suit bottoms. To go with the trousers, the only jacket on offer was a Christian Dior blazer. The latter was at the special 50% discounted price of $300. But they managed to get just enough clothing for normal day use. The problem came with having absolutely nothing suitable for the really formal dinners.

Gradually everybody on board got to learn of the loss of luggage and were sympathetic but, more than anything, relieved that it hadn't happened to them!

Bob was a member of a Lodge in the UK and it was the custom on the QE2, as on most other cruise ships, to arrange a special meeting for Freemasons as well as separate meetings for Rotarians, Lions and Round Table members. There was no formal meeting for Masons as such but plans would be put in place for a special Ladies' Night. A president for the function would be elected and a pre-dinner cocktail party arranged where the Ship's captain and senior staff were the principal guests. The object of the exercise was to endeavour to raise a decent sum for a charity nominated by the Captain. This was almost invariably the RNLI.

Bob, being the most senior member there, was elected to be President but he declined because of the lack of suitable clothing for both Maisie and himself.

At that first planning meeting had been an Indian doctor who offered the use of any of his clothing for Bob and that of his wife's for Maisie. Sadly, neither were of the same build so that advantage could not be taken of their kindness.

Came the big evening with some sixty people present. The president looked the part and his wife, holding a magnificent bouquet of flowers, was beautifully dressed. Guests were welcomed as they arrived and introduced to the Captain and his senior officers. Suddenly, the door opened and in walked the Indian doctor and his wife dressed in shorts and beach wear. They didn't want Bob and Maisie to be embarrassed by being the only ones so dressed.

As it happens, Bob and Maisie had managed to borrow a bit here and a bit there and didn't look too much out of place – which left just the doctor and his wife standing out from the crowd. Bob and his wife offered to go back and change into their beachwear but this was completely unnecessary. The Doctor and his wife were hailed as absolute heroes and treated as real celebrities. Their kindness justly spread around the ship like wildfire. Several other members were only disappointed that they, too, had not thought to come in similar attire to support the pair without luggage.

The ship arrived in Southampton. Bob and Maisie wore their new purchases with their beach clothes in a small plastic bag. They also carried the large quilt.

As they arrived at immigration, they were stopped by the officer in charge who took one look at what they were carrying and said: "We can't let you off the ship without your luggage? Where is it?"

Bob said: "We'd very much like to know that ourselves!"

Their three cases arrived back in the UK some six weeks later. Judging by the variety of labels attaching to it, it appeared to have been round the world twice on a various airlines.

Duck Shooting

Jeremy Russell came from a very privileged family which had an estate in Scotland. By family tradition, he spent much of his adult life in the Royal Navy where he reached the exalted rank of Commander. Although his many decorations showed that he had been involved in active service, he was reluctant to ever make mention of this.

He found himself retired from duty at the age of 58 and had bought a very nice detached property at Westerham for his wife and two of his sons - who were yet to find partners.

Although he had an excellent pension and had no need to work, he felt he needed something to keep his brain active. He was delighted, therefore, to be offered the post of Pensions Representative for a life assurance company based in the City.

It was in that capacity that he came into contact with insurance broker Harry Johnson who had an office based in Gravesend. They became good friends and Jeremy called into see Harry whenever he was in the area. Sometimes they even discussed business.

Over lunch one day, Jeremy said that he was keen on duck shooting and asked if Harry had any knowledge of local areas that might prove useful. The reply was that Cliff Marshes had its fair share of ducks but that he had never participated personally. Jeremy invited Harry to join him one day to check out the area as a possibility and have a day's shooting there.

Harry had no guns at all but Jeremy, at 6'4" in height and with long arms, said he had had two guns presented to him for his 21st birthday.

These had been tailor made as the stocks would be too short on standard guns. He had a '12 bore' – the type used by farmers and shooters of game generally - and an '8 bore'. Harry had never even heard of an '8 bore' previously but Jeremy explained that this gun was very powerful and, when filled with a cartridge instead of shot, could bring down an elephant.

Jeremy had also a '410' shot gun and he suggested that Harry used that as it was light and had a standard length stock. It had only one barrel and was good for somebody with limited experience with guns.

The day out produced absolutely nothing. The ducks were always at a safe distance and it became obvious that a great deal of study would be necessary to stand any chance of hitting any. The ducks seemed to know that nobody with any sporting sense would fire on a duck whilst it was on the ground or on water. They appeared to be either a few yards away floating on the water waiting for somebody to throw them some bread or in flight a quarter of a mile away.

This all represented something of a challenge to the two hunters. One day a week for some three weeks was spent crawling through ditches and hiding behind dykes to plot the flight of the ducks in the area. Harry enjoyed every minute. It was something new and very venturesome to him. He felt close to nature.

Ducks are quite predictable creatures in that they follow the same course 'home' every evening and leave at the same time every morning for their 'day out'. So, came the fourth week, the plan was in place.

The two would go down to the marshland late afternoon to find the birds swimming on their favourite lake. Jeremy would stand to the lea side of them and let fire in the air with his '8 bore'. This would be terribly noisy and would cause the birds to rise and fly in a large circle until they made their way back to their home base. Hopefully, Jeremy might have time also to let off two shots with his '12 bore' once the birds were airborne. Along their line of flight home, Harry would lie low until the birds came overhead when he would let fly with his '410'.

It all worked well. Jeremy fired his '8 bore' in the air and the birds all took off. They did not circle as was hoped but flew in formation towards their home ground. This meant that the birds were virtually out of range by the time that Jeremy had changed guns. Firing at them might result in merely injuring some of the birds – which no person with a conscience would wish.

Harry, on the other hand couldn't have selected a better position and, at the appropriate time, he let fly a single shot. This brought down the bird at which he aimed. A '410' at distance is useless so he didn't get off a second shot.

With some excitement and more than a little trepidation he went to find the bird he had brought down. Questions ran through his mind: What if the bird were not dead? Suppose it was still alive and just looked up at him? Harry reached the bird and it was dead all right. Dead as a dodo. There was a single trickle of blood running down the beautiful coloured neck of the bird. Harry felt absolutely dreadful. How on earth could he harm such a wonderful creature?

Jeremy arrived on the scene and was delighted for Harry. "What a magnificent shot!"

Harry gave the gun back to Jeremy and vowed that never again would he ever kill another creature with a gun. Jeremy was very understanding and assured Harry that the next time they went out shooting it would be ok. He would by then have enjoyed eating the first bird and made sense of it all. Harry was not impressed. He could not eat the bird and never again went shooting. Well, not at least until, as a territorial soldier, he was later summoned for military service in Uganda. But that was a different story.

Saturday Session

For what he claimed were his obvious sins in a previous life, Robbie managed to get lumbered each year in organising the Annual Weekend Conference for his Rotary District. It was usually at Eastbourne with about 1,500 attendees - comprising 750 members and their partners.

In reality, it was not a particularly onerous task provided that preparation started the day after the previous conference had finished. If there were even a short delay, there would be a panic to find suitable speakers because all the decent ones were usually engaged at least a year in advance.

The one session which required special attention was the Saturday afternoon. It was customary to have events of a social nature to relieve the tension of some of the business sessions. The important thing was the requirement that the guests enjoyed themselves before the formal dinner in the evening.

Over the years, there had been golf sessions, bus rides to see the surrounding countryside, fishing competitions, theatre trips and the like. The difficulty was to find something new.

Robbie came up with the idea of laying on a fashion show for the ladies - which Marks and Sparks had kindly agreed to organise. Of course, the men would want something different, so Robbie decided on a wine-tasting party. There would be a limit on numbers to around 700 for each event. But there were always some who just wanted to go shopping, fishing or swimming, so that just the two functions should work out right number-wise.

Accordingly, invitations were sent out asking attendees which of the two events they would like to attend. This is where the problems started. No less than 600 of the women and 650 of the men decided on the wine tasting. Believe it or not, 50 men wanted to go to the fashion show. But one might well be forgiven for thinking that these were ordered by their wives to go with them. The only fair way of dealing with the number problem was to say that 350 men and 350 women could go to the wine-tasting and that the remainder could do their own thing, attend the fashion show or go to the local cinema. Robbie had managed to obtain 50 tickets at a greatly reduced price. Funnily enough, these tickets were all taken quickly as the film showing had received good publicity. Everybody seemed happy with the arrangements.

As M & S were handling the arrangements for the fashion show, it was only necessary to check that everything was in hand so that concentration could be given to the wine-tasting.

One of Robbie's friends, Peter White, often gave talks on wine so his assistance was requested. He suggested that there should be six wines. Three of these would come from France and the other three of the same variety from the new world wine producing areas.

With any luck, they should get eight glasses of wine from each bottle. After all, it was only for tasting and spitting out. To allow for spillages and some more enthusiastic drinkers, it was decided to buy 100 bottles of each wine – 600 bottles in all. All the wine was purchased accordingly in France and brought back by car on several trips.

The next problem was in the provision of spittoons. Where on earth was he going to get these? A local shop manager came to his aid by offering to provide 40 large and used ice cream tubs. These were gratefully accepted.

One of Robbie's local supermarkets agreed to cut up 45lbs of cheddar cheese into 1" cubes and provide 200 packets of dry biscuits for the cleansing of the pallet between wines.

So, it was all sections go. There would be 70 tables each holding ten people with a wine steward appointed for each table to pour the wine to be tasted.

Came the big day, all was ready and organised. The wine, spittoons, cheese, biscuits and glasses were in position and the stewards made aware of their duties. There was also sufficient paper for participants to make notes plus a few pencils for those without writing implements.

The plan was that Peter would be talking about each wine and inviting people to taste it. They could then write down their comments as to which they preferred. The comments would be collected at the end of the session. There would be a prize for the best paper received.

Robbie introduced Peter and there was a hush while he described the procedure and the first wine. After five minutes, one of two in the audience got a bit impatient just gazing at their empty glasses and decided to sample the wine. When they did so, everybody decided to follow suit. The private conversations began. The noise increased and gathered momentum until nobody could hear what Peter was saying at all.

He looked at Robbie who simply shrugged his shoulders. He could not have been heard even if he had tried.

Peter just said "Enjoy yourselves" and sat down. What followed was almost chaos. The noise in the hall was absolutely deafening as the wine flowed and flowed but, instead of spitting out the samples into the spittoons, everybody drank the full glass.

Within fifteen minutes, it was like an office party with half a dozen different conversations on each table with each table competing with the next to make itself heard.

What a wonderful time they all had. The ladies in particular, having drunk six glasses of wine, were in full spirits and there was disappointment all round when the time came for the closing of the session. Everybody said it was the finest conference they have ever attended and, at the end of the day, six people out of the 700 present handed in their notes as to their preference for one wine or another. One plastic spittoon contained some wine but the rest were empty.

The only problem was sobering up for the formal dinner which was to follow two hours later. Fifty-seven people didn't attend. Obviously, they must have caught a cold or something whilst swimming in the sea or, more likely, the excitement of the fashion show proved too much for them.

Truth Will Out

The topic of conversation of a group of employees over Friday lunch would always be the weekend's activities. These would range from the sublime to the ridiculous.

Two of the group, Paul and Tony, would be meeting at the local leisure centre at 7.0 am on the Saturday morning for a few rather frantic exercises in the gym. These would be followed by a few lengths of the pool and half an hour chatting in the steam room. Then would come the huge English breakfast in the restaurant. For certain, the calories lost on exercising would be rather quickly replaced by the second slice of sizzling bacon and black pudding. Still, it all sounded very commendable when the breakfast was omitted from the telling. Sunday for each would be spent in the garden if the weather were good or watching the television if it were not.

Mike and Peter would meet up at first light for a round of golf. This was permitted by their ever-loving wives - who also worked full-time - provided that they were back for lunch at noon and then to accompany them to the supermarket to replenish supplies for the coming week. While their husbands were playing, the wives would have an extra well-deserved lie-in. All four would be going out for lunch on the Sunday as usual at a local pub which served excellent food.

Eric and Tom impressed nobody with their casual D-I-Y/gardening plans for the Saturday. But what followed every Sunday did. Come rain, snow or sun, the two joined an intrepid group of five maniacal swimmers who, at 8.0 am, took a quick dip in the sea – irrespective of weather conditions. This sounded better in the summer months than it did in February when the sea close to where they lived virtually froze over. Nobody could work out how they ever survived this pointless exercise – but survive they did.

Micky, being a bachelor, played every day as it came. That particular Saturday he was going to be out with friends to a show in London followed by dinner and, on the Sunday, he had been invited to a boat ride and lunch in Maidstone.

And then there was Harold. Harold was their company's representative. He would always be out and about somewhere or another with an exciting programme.

The group always waited with baited breath to know what Harold had planned for that weekend. You could bet your last cent that it would be rather more adventuresome than what the others had organised. Without giving too many details, he would usually mention quite casually that he would be off somewhere on his cruiser or be flying to some exotic destination to meet up with old school friends. Some felt that Harold always exaggerated his activities. They took much of what he said with a pinch of salt - particularly when the subject involved the Mediterranean and Malta.

"Ah, yes", he would say, "This weekend we may well be taking a cruise in the Med and popping into Malta - if time permits. We'll be thinking of you all as we sit there over lunch with a bottle of red followed by a double brandy with our coffee! It's nice to get these weekend breaks away. It makes such a difference going off somewhere on a Friday evening and coming back late on Sunday night. Marvellous! And the women you meet are always good company! Helps me overcome the labours of the previous week."

Micky and his friend, Alan, left Maidstone at noon on the Sunday and they headed off down the river to the pub where the lunch had been booked by his host.

On arrival, much to Micky's surprise he found Harold with his pint of beer relating some of his exotic tales.

"Hello Harold" said Micky, "I didn't expect to find you here." Harold's face dropped like a stone.

"Ah, Micky. I didn't expect to see you here either. Didn't know you were a boating man. Do you get down the river often?"

"As it happens, I don't - but my friend, Alan here, brought me down in his boat for lunch. Alan, this is one of my work colleagues, Harold. He's always got an interesting tale to tell. I must confess that I have been seriously considering getting a small craft, for Harold is always telling us what fun he has on his on the River Medway and the Malta Inn - or the Med and Malta, as I think you prefer to call them, Harold! Being a novice at these things, I haven't got the faintest idea of what I should buy. Perhaps I could take look at yours some time. I take it that you are moored outside. Which one is yours?"

Harold put his arm around Micky's shoulder and pulled him to one side outside the hearing of the group of people.

"Well, to be completely honest, old boy, I don't have a boat any more. When Lloyds' collapsed a few years ago, I lost absolutely everything. The house, the boat, my villa in Sicily and even my wife, Sonia. All went. I was left with virtually nothing. I had to borrow from a friend to even get the deposit on a small flat I wanted to buy.

"Since then I have been struggling to meet the mortgage repayments. Frankly, I make up all those stories because I can't bear the shame of what has happened. I suppose the game is up now and I shall have to come clean next Friday. I hate to think what the lads will make of it. It might be better if you told them. I hate the idea of having to face them."

Mickey looked at Harold and immediately felt quite sorry for him. For Harold the game really was up and that could make him the laughing stock of the office when, in reality, he was just hiding his misfortune from others.

When the next Friday came round, they all listened carefully as to what the others were doing but, when it was Harold's turn, Micky stepped in and said:

"Do you mind if I tell them about last weekend, Harold?" and, before Harold could reply, Micky continued:

"Although Harold was planning to go off to his old hunting ground, the truth must come out. I talked him into coming with me down the River Medway last Sunday to look at some boats. I am hoping to buy one shortly. But I know nothing about them at all. Harold has got rid of his boat with a view to getting something bigger a bit later. He has kindly agreed to give me some instructions on what to buy and how to steer the thing. I don't think Harold really knows what a full-time job he has taken on. So wish him luck with his new venture. I hate to think where we shall finish up – somewhere in the Med and, who knows, we might even pop in to Malta! We shall think of you all when we are sitting in the sun with a few glasses of red!"

Micky turned round and saw Harold fighting back the tears.

Golden Rays

Harry and Mary were a very happily married couple. They did more than their fair share of socialising but they were not ones to have a party at the drop of a hat. They would much prefer a dinner for two at the local pub when it came to birthdays and the like.

However, their 50th wedding anniversary was fast approaching. Most of their friends and relations were aware of this and wondered what they would do by way of a celebration.

Harry said "We just went on a cruise on our own for our ruby wedding anniversary. They will never forgive us if we repeat that. Fred from next door has said already that everybody was waiting with baited breath as to what we were planning. I guess we are a bit stuck with doing something, Mary. But what?"

Mary responded by saying "The problem will be sheer numbers. If we invite your brother and sister that would mean inviting my three sisters, their husbands and kids. Before we knew what hit us we should have about 17 relations alone. Then, of course there are Jack and Barbara, Rita and Fred, Alan and Margaret. Oh, dear, it just goes on and on. That's without our neighbours in the flats! If we were to invite Shirley and Dick that would mean inviting the other 16!"

"Yes, the cost of inviting that lot out to a formal dinner would be more than a Caribbean cruise! I suppose we could take them down the road to the pub. But I don't think they would like that much. Remember how they complained about the inedible pork chops when Sarah had her bash there?"

"Perhaps if we were to split them into two groups that might help. We could then possibly be able to cope with it here in the flat. With a bit of thought, we could lay on a nice buffet."

"Well, that sounds a good idea to me. Let's invite the neighbours first. They won't have to drive so they will just bash into the wine - as usual. They won't be too worried about food just as long as the wine keeps flowing! So we don't really need to worry about what we have to eat and what quantity. If we find we do have problems at that do, we can correct them for when the family come. Because they are driving they won't be drinking so will expect something extra special by way of eats."

"That's what we'll do then. We'll have the neighbours on Sunday, 23rd, and the others on the following Sunday, 30th. Just a minute, though, if we held it on 24th and the other on 31st, the chances are that some couldn't come because of getting time off work. That would cut down the numbers a bit. It is not knowing whose coming is what is worrying me most."

Harry assured her that it would be all right. "I'll run off some invitations on the computer saying that neighbours should come, if possible, on 24th and relatives on 31st. But, if they couldn't manage one date, they would be welcome to come on the other one. That would make them feel really wanted. I'll also put on the invitation that the functions will be from 12.30 pm to 2.30 pm. That will make sure that it doesn't go on and on."

Mary responded "That sounds good to me. Let's go for it! I reckon that, with a bit of luck, we could get around ten at each do and we could cope with that without any problems."

Harry sent out the invitations asking for an RSVP so as to get the number for each date.

Things didn't go quite according to plan. Most of the people who accepted the invitation said that they could only manage 31st. Quite a number apologised because of holidays, prior engagements or simply couldn't get time off from work.

"So, how many do you think we shall have then Harry?" posed Mary.

"Well, it's beginning to look as though we shall have about fourteen coming on 31st and just four on 24th. I suggest that we just scrub 24th completely. Some are bound to have colds or something at the last minute so the number won't be too far away. In any case, we can't be sure that those four will be able to make 31st. Let's just take a chance and, if we have a couple of extras, it won't matter too much."

"You'll have to tell the four who could manage the 24th," said Mary. She then added: "In fact, we had better tell everybody that it is now only on 31st otherwise people may just turn up on the off-chance on 24th."

They both agreed that it sounded good and another problem was sold. They packed themselves on the back for their great planning and started to organise the menu for the big day.

As it came nearer, the congratulatory cards arrived in great numbers. When the count came to 55 cards, both Harry and Mary started to feel they were being a bit mean about the whole thing. They began to wish that they had placed a higher value on friendship. But what could they do at that late stage? Get another venue? Change the date back to the weekend? They could think of nothing that was realistic in the time frame available. What was done was done and they would have to live with it.

They decided to scrap the cheap wine and buy some decent champagne. They would upgrade the menu in both quality and quantity.

"Let's really lay on something special. Shall I order a big cake?"

"Yes, do that. And perhaps we can ask the folk who apologised to come to lunch in pairs later in the year."

That's good. I beginning to feel better now about the whole thing. Let's make it a true celebration of our 50 years together!"

The great day arrived and the bouquets of flowers arrived by the cart load along with another ten anniversary cards.

The guests arrived just after noon bringing with them champagne, chocolates, other gifts and even more flowers. People were arriving who had previously apologised - explaining that they just could not miss the big day. They hoped it would be all right.

The numbers grew and grew until both Harry and Mary got separated in the crowd. It was standing room only.

Harry caught sight of Mary and asked if she realised that 35 people had arrived so far. "Thirty-five?" she questioned – "I made it 39!" In reality both were wrong. The actual number in attendance was 43 - as people not even invited just popped in to wish them well!

Being family and friends, everybody chipped in to help out with the work. Three of the men were pouring drinks for everybody. Others squeezed between the guests with plates of sandwiches, pizzas, drumsticks, quiche and the like.

It was soon obvious that sandwiches were going to be in short supply. Mary fought her way to the kitchen only to find that some of the guests were already hard at work preparing some more. Neighbours had even gone back to their own flats to get some extra bread and bits and pieces to help out.

The drinks, too, were rapidly disappearing. But that was no problem. There were plenty of bottles of champagne brought by the guests and some of these had already been put in the fridge to chill them before being served. Harry and Maisie were allowed to do nothing.

With great difficulty to be heard above the endless noise, at 3.0 o'clock, the toast to the happy couple was proposed by one of their neighbours, Tom. He paid tribute to such a wonderful and generous couple. This was greeted with loud cheers and applause.

That, however, was not the end of the function but merely a break in proceedings. People did start to drift away around 6.0 pm with hugs and kisses to the happy couple. The last few, who had been battling with the mountain of washing up, left at 7 o'clock.

Then there was silence. Harry and Mary just stood there looking at one another with tears in their eyes. People had been so good and they had been so mean.

The silence was broken by Harry who said: "What about another do for your birthday the week after next? I think we might just have some champagne left!"

Erith Squash Club

There was one very big drawback to being the last people of an evening to play squash on the courts at the local cricket club; that was the closing-up arrangements.

You could book courts only one week in advance. As people left the court, they booked for the same time the following week. If they didn't do so, their time would probably be lost for ever.

Bob, Alan, Ron and Tony played regularly at 9.45 pm every Wednesday. This meant coming off court at around 10.30 pm, having a shower before going up to the bar to pour themselves a drink and placing the money in the till. By 11 o'clock everybody wanted to go home. The procedure was that the last players took all the money from the till and placed it in an envelope. They then, turned off the power to the shower unit, set the burglar alarm, turned off the lights and locked up the place. On the way home, the envelope containing the money and the club keys were pushed through the Treasurer's letterbox. He lived close by.

To say that this arrangement was 'a pain in the bottom' understated the situation!

Every Wednesday, the moans went on until one night Fred said: "I'm fed up to the teeth with this arrangement. I wonder how much it would cost to build our own club."

He expected hoots of laughter but, instead, everybody took the question seriously. Bob said that he would try to find out. The following week he reported that 'Banburys' could build a court for £40,000 but that would not include the land.

He then had asked a couple of friends on the local council if they knew of any land going. They found a site in a very poor area of the town which was not really suitable for either housing or shops. If they were to put forward a serious offer, the Council would almost certainly let them have it because it was an eyesore at present.

The site was on a small road leading to a warehouse on the banks of the River Thames. Large rolls of paper used for printing Newspapers were unloaded from ships and stored there until required. A lorry collection was made once a day.

The four wood-be owners of the squash club worked out that they could build a six court complex on the site for around £250,000. This figure would·include two saunas, a large lounge area and a 34 seater restaurant. They planned to offer the Council £5,000 a year rent for a 21 year lease. The lease would be subject to rent review every seven years but contain the option of their buying the freehold.

Tony was charged with having a word with his local friendly bank manager who said that, if the four each raised £25,000, with their personal guarantees he would lend the company £150,000.

Strange as it may seem, the figures all worked out well. There was not another club within five miles and there was a long waiting list to obtain membership. If they charged each member £10 per month and they took 300 members that would give them sufficient income to meet the regular outgoings. But, of course, there would be a good income from the bar and the restaurant. In addition, there would be a charge for discos in the lounge and for the use of the sun beds which would be installed. They planned to have a couple of slot machines which should raise a substantial sum each year in addition.

After two months, the lease was signed, plans were in place and ground works commenced. It was estimated that the work would take only four months as much of the building would be prefabricated.

Of course, there were problems. The first of these was when the JCB was digging out ground for the foundation. There was a loud clanging noise when it struck a huge underground pipe which proved to be the main gas supply to the town centre. Fortunately, there was no damage to the pipe and the only comment from the Gas Board was "We wondered where that pipe was!" Apparently, it was very old and they had no plans showing its exact location. This meant moving the building three feet to one side of where it was originally planned.

Another problem was that the same JCB broke through the mains water supply to a neighbouring building. As this was the local Working Men's Club, there was intense pressure to get it fixed. It took three days to undertake the work because a completely new pipe had to be laid some 200 feet.

There was also the occasion when the JCB struck what appeared to be a concrete manhole cover. This turned out to be a 30 feet deep Victorian well which served the house which stood on the site at the time. The water at the bottom of the well was completely pure and it was thought that it might prove to be a good architectural feature. The surveyor thought otherwise and ordered it to be filled with a mixture of sand and cement.

But, with all the difficulties, the building was finished on schedule and it looked absolutely magnificent. It had many attractive features. One of these was having a large car park. But a heavy chain had to be placed across the entrance to prevent over-night parking by outsiders.

There were two last jobs to be undertaken. The first was to plant 18 trees inside the boundary to hide the hideous corrugated iron fence. The second was to lay the flowering plants in the garden and, in addition, to put in situ two bay trees in pots on either side of the entrance. They left that night after the work was completed and there was great excitement about the formal opening by the mayor the very next day.

On arrival the following morning, they found the chain across the entrance had been cut and taken away by the local tearaways. Twelve of the 18 trees had been uprooted and stolen along with one of the bay trees – complete with its concrete pot. (As it happens, the remaining trees and pot were stolen the following night.)

All this proved terribly disappointing but the place still looked magnificent and the mayor accompanied by other dignitaries were most impressed. There was a good write-up the following day in the local press.

It was almost impossible to cope with the applications for membership which simply poured in. The Erith Squash Club was duly established.

The next four years showed a regular increase in membership and it soon became the rule that new applications could only be accepted to replace those members who left.

The £10 per month paid by members each month meant that they did not pay for courts in addition. This arrangement suited those who played regularly but not so much those who were infrequent attenders. The latter had no alternative but to pay the £10 as there was no other option open to them.

Then came the bitter blow. Having seen the success of the Squash Club, the Local Council decided to build its own just two miles away. The subscription there was just £15 a year plus £2 whenever you played. This arrangement suited many and quite a number resigned to take up Council membership.

The reduced membership hit the Club badly for the drop in income placed a heavy burden on the Directors. So much so that it was decided to copy the example set by the Council on charges. The regular players objected strongly to the change and several left on principle to join yet another Club which was opened two miles away in the opposite direction to that of the Council's. There were now three clubs operating in the same area fighting for members.

Surprisingly, and completely out of the blue, a new Macdonalds restaurant opened up on the other side of the road from the Club and everybody was asking how on earth they expected to make a profit in such a poor location.

The Club was no longer a good fund-raiser for the Directors – each of whom had his own business to run - and it began to take up more time than each was prepared to devote to it. Reluctantly, the Directors decided to sell the club but, with such strong competition, who would be willing to buy it? Fortunately, one of the club members said he felt he could make a go of it by using the restaurant for group functions. The sale went through at the original cost price so there was no financial loss.

It was not long before the mystery of the Macdonalds restaurant opening deepened when the new owner of the Squash Club purchased the freehold of the site from the local authority. The club was flattened and the land sold to the KFC restaurant chain for a substantial sum.

Just what was happening in this quiet town? All soon became clear. A new and extremely large Morrison's Superstore – complete with petrol pumps – opened just 100 yards from the Squash Club on the site of the paper warehouse. The town suddenly became alive with the throngs of busy shoppers from the surrounding area. So who knew what then?

Eye to Eye

Information on who makes and sells what is freely available on the net. But there is always the fear when dealing with somebody new that nothing is known of the business. A question mark hangs over its reliability, the quality of the product, the type of people concerned and the way it operates. For this reason many companies in the Bexley area were purchasing goods and services from companies often many miles away. A company offering the same goods or services were often literally just a few hundred yards away on a neighbouring industrial estate. But the same question always arose: 'What do we know of them?' Invariably the answer to the question was 'Nothing'.

So, to overcome these problems, the 'Industry to Industry' (or 'Eye to Eye') programme came into being. It was the brainchild of two local businessmen, the brothers Rob and Andrew Perkins. The local authority seized the opportunity to become involved and claim it as its own.

Once a month, a different business would offer a tour of inspection of its premises followed by a buffet lunch and a question time. Businesses would have the opportunity of seeing exactly what their neighbours were offering and the type of people concerned. This scheme proved to be very popular and it certainly encouraged local trading.

One local industry undertook the production of oil by crushing peanuts and coconut shells. The oil was used to make such items as soap, face cream and other cosmetics and, of course, for cooking. The nuts were stored in huge silos on the banks of the River Thames. These were replenished regularly by shipments from Africa.

When Rob was still at school, he belonged to an economics group which studied unusual businesses and had arranged for a to visit this particular factory.

Some forty years after his first visit, Rob led the local businessmen on a tour of the works. Since Rob was last there, additional silos had been added to the previous four. These prevented the situation of running out of stock at any one time of the raw materials through shipping and other delays. Rob was the only person there who had known the plant as it was.

On the latest visit, Rob asked the Works Manager, John Baker, if the silos were still fully utilised.

"Fully utilised? Those silos have been completely empty for years" replied John.

"If you don't mind my asking, where do you store the nuts then?"

"That's easy" came the reply. "We don't use nuts any more. We now crush solely rape seed. This is delivered to us direct from farms several times a day. We then crush the seeds and deliver the oil immediately."

Rob responded "Well, of course, that's the modern way of doing things. I think they call it JIT Management, don't they? Why pay for materials months in advance when you don't have to? The trouble is, though, the farmers have to store the seed and don't get paid until after it is delivered. That's a bit hard on them isn't it?"

"Yes, Just-in-time Management can be tough on the smaller suppliers but we try not to keep them waiting for their money. Because we buy in such bulk, we do have the whip hand but we treat them with the same respect as we demand from the buyers of our oil. We all have to work together"

"Of course, a lot of firms aren't like that, are they? They keep their suppliers waiting for ages for their money but yet demand immediate payment from the purchasers of the goods. Often they actually get the money in before they have paid for their suppliers. Nice work if you can get it!"

Rob always entertained some doubt as to the morality of JIT Management and, notwithstanding the reputation of this particular company for fair play, the visit did little to gain his approval of the general principles involved and the pressure it places on the smaller businesses.

Within a week, he heard on the BBC News that diesel drivers all over the country were on strike and that transport had ground to a halt virtually everywhere.

"I wonder how they are getting on with their factory at a standstill. No rape seed in and no oil out!" said Rob to Andrew with a grin. It might have been a good idea to have at least one of those silos filled with seed to meet such a contingency. There can be drawbacks to JIT Management, you know!"

Flower Man

When you met Harry Robertson for the first time, you couldn't help but take to him immediately. He was a jovial man in his late sixties who always greeted everybody with a warm smile and an extended hand in friendship. You felt you had known him for years. His accent intimated that he was from the London area but doubts were cast on this immediately because of his command of the English language and the way he used it to such advantage.

He was by trade a wholesale florist. This involved his being in London at the crack of dawn each day to receive supplies from the growers before selling them to retail outlets.

His success came because he was a natural businessman. He was liked equally by vendors and purchasers. The price would rarely be the lowest but both the service and the quality could never be faulted – especially when coupled with the reliability one could place on him.

His command of the English language came from his constant reading which also made him a mine of information on the remotest of subjects. Because of this, he was always a favourite when people were taking part in quizzes. Somehow, Harry always finished up on the winning team which, in his usual manner, he claimed was because of the other members of it and not his personal contribution. He was so genuinely modest.

Most would describe Harry as a passive individual and a truly gentle person with a heart of solid gold. But what they did not know was that his many hidden talents were soon recognised by the Army when he was called up for military service during WW2. Within months of his joining he was recruited into the SAS.

He was a member of the Special Raiding Squadron which blew up three German airfields in Libya destroying some 60 enemy aircraft followed by desperate fighting in Italy and Sicily. In 1950 he was first involved in the Korean War and then in various activities in Malaya. Harry was a born killer and his assassinations were both swift and soundless. He was the one they sent in first to immobilise the guards; a swift arm round the throat and the penetration of his knife in the spine was more often than not the solution to a problem. He was alert and reliable to the nth degree.

By all means take his hand when extended to you in friendship but it might be better for you not to approach him quietly from the rear for, although he is now a retired gentleman, his reactions tend to be both automatic and deadly even to this day.

Highgate Amateur Dramatic Society

Planning started for the next Christmas pantomime almost immediately the previous one closed. It was decided that 'Dick Whittington' would be the next production. The only problem that could be foreseen was that two of the usual leading participants would not be available to take on the major roles. They both felt that they were a little past their 'sell-by date'.

As the months passed, this minor problem became more and more important for nobody wanted to take on the leading positions.

Tony had been a member of the Society for some years and, although he had had a few 'walk-on' parts, he was mainly in charge of scenery and assisting the stage manager generally.

His offer to take on the main character received a mixed reception for he had neither the build nor the personality the character required. However, when the situation narrowed down to become a choice between Tony or paying for a professional actor, he got the role.

Faith in Tony's ability to fulfil the role diminished with each rehearsal. But the good news was that a couple of new members had shown much promise. They could well become leading characters in future productions. Indeed, one of them, Peter, agreed to be an understudy to Tony for this production.

A rehearsal just one week before the show was due to open justified previous concerns. It proved to be the biggest disaster yet for Tony.

From the outset, he had all the words but the jokes and general dialogue fell completely flat. He apologised profusely and said that he was not feeling well.

Somebody suggested that, rather than burden Tony, why not ask Peter to take over the role for at least the opening performance. All agreed that this might be the best course. Tony felt so poorly that he readily agreed. He would simply swop roles with Peter immediately at that rehearsal.

Peter was absolutely brilliant and put Tony to shame. At the end, Peter received a long round of applause from the other players – including Tony who continued when the others had finished.

The reality was that everybody, without exception, felt terribly sorry for Tony. He had worked so hard on the part. But the show really did need to be a success or that could badly affect future productions.

Came the opening night. Tony walked slowly to his place at the side of the stage when the production manager called out to him: 'What do you think you are doing?"

"I'm just standing by in my role as the understudy for Peter" replied Tony.

"Oh, no you aren't, we have just this minute had a phone call from Peter saying that has gone down with the same bug that you had. We have been waiting for you to arrive. You are taking the main role right now. Off to the changing room immediately."

Tony's heart skipped a few beats as he hastened to get changed. He got a pat on the back for encouragement and good luck as he walked towards the stage dressed for his part.

Well, luck he didn't need. Having seen how Peter had played the part at rehearsal had given Tony a new lease of life. He copied Peter to the letter. And the result? A standing ovation at the end of the show and a big kiss from the leading lady who was, in fact, Peter's wife.

Check-Mate

Perhaps it would not be fair to say that Leslie Mackrell was the worst driver in the world. But the chances are that he would certainly run a very close second. Certainly this was the view of the police when they attended an accident in the High Street involving Leslie's car.

This had struck a parked, unoccupied van. Not unreasonably, Leslie blamed the owner of the car for parking in a bay without paying the parking fee. The police did not take this view and preferred charges against him.

After the Court hearing, Leslie was all smiles as he left the Court.

"You look happy, Les. How did you get on?" enquired Dick, who was a close friend of his.

"Well, they preferred a number of charges against me but they didn't stick."

"Didn't stick?"

"No. But they did say that further charges may follow at a later date."

"I don't want to be unkind but I should have thought that it was an open and shut case against you, Leslie."

"No" was the reply. "In fact it turned out that they were in a bit of trouble."

"What trouble can the Court be in?"

"Well, it was the way that the bloke drew up the charges" continued Leslie.

"The first charge said that I was driving without 'L' plates while the holder of a provisional licence. They then added: driving without insurance while the holder of a provisional licence and, thirdly, that I was driving unaccompanied while the holder of a provisional licence."

"What was wrong with those charges that they were dropped?"

"I pleaded 'not guilty' and they asked me the grounds on what I did so as I had already admitted that I hadn't passed the driving test. Well, I just told them that I hadn't got a licence of any kind – provisional or otherwise.

"The chairman looked at the other two on the bench. They simply shrugged their shoulders and the case was dismissed! They weren't very happy about it and asked to see the person who drew up the charges. I wouldn't want to be in his shoes!

"The police were waiting for me as I walked from the dock to 'have a few words' as they put it. But they were happy after we made the deal."

"What was that then?" Dick enquired.

"I simply told them the truth that I was suffering from macular degeneration. This meant that I couldn't pass the driving test with my eyesight even if I knew the Highway Code – which I didn't. They obviously felt a bit sorry for me and we made the agreement that, as from today, they just didn't want to see me in a vehicle in the area ever again. If they did, they would throw the book at me and ensure that I finished up 'inside'. I told them that, with my eyesight, I couldn't see them either. So we called it 'thirty all' and shook hands on the deal.

Harry's Decanter

Harry Jeffery and his wife, Paula, were invited out probably more than most to a variety of functions. Undoubtedly, the reason for this was that Harry could always be relied upon to propose a toast or reply on behalf of the guests with great aplomb at little or no notice. He had a knack of knowing just what was right for any particular occasion. He would have the audience in fits of laughter at a wedding but was equally at home with a great sense of sympathy and understanding at a funeral or with sense of decorum on an official occasion.

Paula, on the other hand, was not much at getting to her feet to speak but was an absolute marvel when it came to private conversations. She would listen intensely to the most boring of topics and everybody considered her to be the ideal companion and wanted to sit next to her.

A City of London Police Commissioner, a Knight of the Realm, sat next to her on one occasion. The conversation was non-stop. So much so that people afterwards wanted to know the subject which enthralled them both. It must be at Government level at least.

The answer, as Harry established on their way home, was the ownership of cats. Paula had had her last cat for some 19 years whilst the Commissioner had at least three cats at any one time. This topic had kept them chatting away throughout the two hour dinner.

There was one occasion where Harry was the guest of honour and he sat next to the President of the local Rotary Club's wife. Just for something to start the conversation, Harry picked up his name place card and commented on how pretty it was. He said jokingly how nice it was when people spelt his surname properly. The president's wife looked at the card in horror and apologised profusely for the incorrect spelling of his name. Harry laughed at her concern and said that people often got it wrong but it was right in on this occasion. Her face dropped noticeably.

"Right?" she asked.

"Yes, perfectly correct. What's wrong, my dear?" asked Harry.

"I'm afraid you will find out soon enough! I'm so sorry.'"

Harry was puzzled but felt he couldn't press the matter.

Later in the evening, the President rose and paid great tribute to Harry. He said he had much pleasure in presenting him "With this engraved decanter to show the appreciation of his members for Harry's support over the years." He then apologised profusely for the misspelling of Harry's surname but that he hoped that it would be possible to have the engraving altered - at the Club's expense, of course.

Harry took it in good part – as only Harry could – and said in his response that he wouldn't dream of having it altered as "It will remind me of those lovely people who presented it to me. After all, who cares about what it says on the outside of a decanter; it's what is in the inside which counts!" The audience loved his reply. To this very day, Harry still has the decanter on display at his home for all to see. He takes great delight in explaining the spelling error.

Harry claimed, rather untruthfully, that he only ever decided what to say when he actually got to a function. He said that he liked to work on the basis that "Something interesting will happen which will provide me with some ammunition."

On one occasion, Harry was invited to reply on behalf of the guests at a black tie dinner for some 250 people at a rather 'posh' hotel in Torquay. He said afterwards that, as he starting to get to his feet, he was still wondering what to say. Suddenly, the door opened at the other end of the room and in walked a workman carrying a toilet pan on his shoulder.

The workman stopped immediately, apologised profusely and backed out of the room highly embarrassed. The audience started to laugh as he appeared to be bowing with every backward step – as though leaving royalty. This got everybody in the right mood to hear Harry speak. He certainly had a subject on which to hang his address that evening. He began:

"That reminds me of the night that my wife and I were in Istanbul. We were invited to a traditional 18 course dinner. The highly respected Sheik Ahmedia of Somalia was the principal guest. He had a bad back and he insisted in having his servants take his special chair along wherever he went. He called the chair his 'travelling throne'. But I can assure you that it wasn't as posh as the one we have just seen."

Harry teased his audience by claiming that he knew most there thought he had actually paid the man to appear with the toilet pan. He went to great lengths to tell everybody that such was not the case but 'accidentally' disclosed how much he had given him. It was non-stop laughter for fifteen minutes before Harry actually got round to the subject of his address – which took approximately three minutes to impart.

Just A Small Job

Ron Parkinson and his partner, Keith Roberts, were highly respected business consultants. One morning, Ron received an unexpected call from a Terry Gardner of Business Link. Terry asked him if he could help out by making a few calls on its behalf on some local businesses. It appeared that several of them had run into trouble and needed some professional advice.

Ron already had a rather busy schedule so, in order to reach a decision, he said he really needed to know a bit more about what was involved. It was all right saying 'local' but he had been caught before by taking on a 'local' job where the head office proved to be 150 miles away. A very long way to travel for a two hour meeting.

"Well, I do have a few questions to ask before I can discuss the matter with my partner, Keith. The first one is, of course, just how many calls have you in mind?"

"We don't really know that just yet" replied Terry "but it can't be many. A list is being prepared by the local Chamber of Commerce and, if you agree to help, this will be sent on to you immediately the details are known."

"The next question is as to what kind of problems do the businesses have? My guess would be that most of them are running out of money!"

"Oh, no. Most would just need a bit of guidance on their future activities. But, of course, this may vary just a little."

"Now you said the businesses were local. Just how local are they?"

"As they are all members of the Chamber of Commerce, they are bound to be within a short distance of each other."

"OK but now comes the crunch: How do we get paid? Will it be by the hour?"

Terry responded: "We reached the conclusion that it would be best to pay you £25 for each call you make. Not a lot I appreciate, but there should not be much involved. The way we operate is that there would be basically three contacts on each business. The first one would be just a few words to determine the problem - which you go away and think about. A few days later you get back in touch with them with your solution. Finally, about three weeks later, you ask them if their problem has been solved. So, in effect, you get £75 per case. I think you will agree that it is not bad for what is likely to be just a few minutes of your time. And, of course, look at the contacts you will be making."

"It doesn't sound very much to me but I take it that we get expenses on top of the £75?"

"Well, we weren't thinking of paying expenses as most of the businesses are probably going to be within walking distance of one another. So, at the most, it would involve you in just the short journey from your office to the first one - which might even be next door! Who knows at this stage?

"Well, I'm sure my partner will agree to my taking this on to help out as a one-off but I have to say that I do have some misgivings. You make it all sound like 'a walk in the park'. Obviously, our job is to help people but it does look as though we are entering into this more than a bit in the dark."

"Don't you worry about it. You will probably find that you will be able to do three or four calls of a morning and probably the same number of an afternoon. Money for old socks really. Only joking, of course!"

"Perhaps we had better wait and see."

A week later, the list of businesses arrived on Ron's desk.

"I really don't believe this." Ron said to Keith. "How would you believe that there are 48 different companies on this list?"

"How many did you say?"

"Forty-eight of the blighters. And, boy, you see where they are located. They may all be in the Chamber's area but some of them are 12 miles away."

They were both horrified at what Terry had landed them with. There was no doubt that Keith would have to do some of them otherwise they would go on for ever.

Ron got back on the phone to Terry.

"Have you seen this list of businesses that's been sent to me?"

"No, that must have come from the Chamber directly to you. What's the problem?"

"Well, not only are there 48 companies on the list but they are miles apart from one another. The first one is three miles down the road from here and the nearest one to that is another two miles further on. This is going to take a month of Sundays to sort out."

"I'm sorry about that but I had no idea of what was involved number-wise. The problem is, I guess, that the service is free to the clients. Quite obviously, the managers of most small businesses are seizing the opportunity of getting free advice from experts. You know, you may be able to deal with some of the enquiries on the phone. I do so hope you are able to help us out as we are knee deep with enquiries from all over the county."

"Well, if we can knock them off quickly, we should be able to cope but I have to say that there is not much hope of that. We've been down this road before. On the surface, it looks a quick 'knock off' job, only to find in reality that the whole business needs to be taken apart and almost re-built from scratch. Of course, the owners don't like to admit that anything is wrong. You know you are in for trouble when the company's accountant joins in the conversation. I'm afraid we have to be quite rude to them at times for the reality is that, if they had done their job properly, the company wouldn't be in a mess. But, I'll be back in touch once we have spent the first couple of days on the job. I really just can't see that we can possibly cope with 48 of them."

"Thanks very much. I'll make sure that we make it up to you in other ways."

"I always get terribly nervous when people say that. It usually means we get more of the same rubbish. Still, let's wait and see what happens."

The very first call that Ron made filled the complete morning. The afternoon call on the same day involved a far larger concern which took the rest of the day and most of the following morning to resolve. The reality was that the problems on every single case were real. Without support, many of those businesses undoubtedly would fail. Ron just couldn't let that happen. If a job was worth doing.......

Working virtually full-time on the project, it took Ron and Keith three weeks to complete the first calls alone; and another month to complete the second and third calls.

Ron left word with his receptionist that: "If either Business Link or the Chamber of Commerce call again doing us favours, we are all out and you don't know when we'll be back!"

Wreck of a Fish

Fishing for conger eels is not the easiest of pastimes. They lurk inside the wreck of sunken ships which have been dispatched to the sea bed by having run-aground, capsized in a storm, been involved in a collision or sunk by enemy action.

Wrecks have one thing in common. They prove a hazard to any ship or boat wishing to anchor in the area. This doesn't help one little bit when a boat is carrying anglers to catch congers. It needs to drop its anchor to prevent the boat drifting off course in a strong wind, tide or current.

The usual method of fishing for congers, therefore, takes the form of anchoring the boat upstream of the wreck and letting out the anchor chain to allow the boat to drift back over the wreck itself. Of course, the loss of fishing tackle can often prove an expensive exercise. This can easily get caught up in the wreckage.

As there are wrecks everywhere, so congers are found in very many locations. Some areas, however, prove to have a larger population of congers than others. One of the most prolific areas is off Brixham in Devon. There are several boats there specialising in taking anglers to selected wrecks along the coastline. One such boat was called 'Our Unity' and another 'Enterprise' – both of which were reported regularly in angling publications as being most successful in their hauls. Often a single conger would weigh in excess of 40 lbs.

Rob and his son, Harry, decided to drive down to Brixham one weekend to try their luck. Unfortunately, both of the boats mentioned

were fully booked so they had to take what they could get. The boat
with room was somewhat ancient and with a skipper to match. They
had hardly left the harbour when the boat developed engine trouble. It
limped the rest of the way out to sea on one engine at about 5 knots -
half its normal speed. In the meantime, 'Our Unity' sped by doing
around 20 knots.

The fishing was slow and not a single conger was hooked, yet alone
landed. There were a couple of black bream and the ubiquitous mackerel
but nothing of any consequence. The skipper explained that he didn't
fish over wrecks any more because he had lost an anchor some time
ago while doing that and, of course, he had to buy some 70 metres of
chain to go with it.

After three hours, it started to blow up rough. The skipper thought
they should return to the harbour. The anchor was hauled up and the
boat started off. It had been going less than fifteen minutes when 'Our
Unity' sped by with four anglers holding up a large conger in each of
their hands. The fish were so large that their tails were dragging on the
deck! All most disappointing for Rob and Harry.

In the meantime, Rob's friend, Pete, who couldn't join the other two
in Brixham, decided to try his luck fishing for flounders at Folkestone.
He drove down in the morning with his 8' dinghy on top of his car.
He was on his own which meant he just about had enough room in
the boat for himself and all his tackle. A boat that size was not really
suitable for use as anything other than a tender to a larger vessel on
inland waterways. But the sea was comparatively calm and he planned
only to go out a couple of hundred yards off shore.

He caught nothing at all in the morning and decided to call it a
day. He pulled up his light anchor but left his fishing line in the water
in the hope of getting a last minute 'bite'.

All of a sudden, he had the most enormous jerk on his line. About
twenty yards of line raced off his reel. When he stopped the line by
gripping the reel handle, the boat started moving through the water. It
was slowly being pulled out to sea.

"What shall I do?" he thought. "Cut the line or drop the anchor? He
decided on the latter. But, as it was a fairly sandy bottom, the anchor

merely dragged through it. All at once, the anchor took hold on what must have been a rock. The anchor rope went tight as the boat jerked to a halt. Pete had no option but to let more line off his reel. It was an experience he didn't expect.

Suddenly the pulling stopped. He started to feel that he had the situation under control as he wound in line on his reel. But, without warning, the line pulled off again and, not only took back the line he had wound in but more as well. He looked at his reel. There was little line left on it. His rod was bent almost double. He fell backwards when the pulling stopped again and the line went completely slack. He wound the line back on his reel as fast as he could waiting all the time for another pull on the line. It didn't come and Peter naturally assumed that whatever was on the line had gone.

Pete found it all quite worrying. What on earth had he hooked? He had heard of a case a short time earlier of an angler hooking a dead body off the bottom and having similar problems when the body wanted to float off in the tide. The problem is always that the tides are often stronger on the seabed than on the surface. A sunken log could also be the trouble. What should he do?

He continued to wind in the line with no resistance at all. Soon the head of a giant conger eel appeared a few yards from his dinghy. He could see that it was about four or five feet in length – perhaps even longer. The line went tight again as the fish made a dash for it pulling line off the reel as it went. But this was short-lived and it was obvious that the conger was exhausted. He gradually wound in the line and pulled the fish to the side of the boat.

But what was he going to do next? These fish have large mouths and razor sharp teeth. The thought of a five feet long eel with him in an 8' boat filled him with absolute dread. He put his gaff in the water and hooked the conger under its gills and, with a large heave, pulled it into the boat.

He realised soon enough that there was not room in the boat for the two of them so, without thinking it through, he jumped into the water holding on to the side. Slowly he made his way round the boat hand over hand to the anchor rope and attempted to raise the anchor. This was quite impossible with just one hand. The boat was almost tipping over with his weight and that of the anchor. There was only one thing to do. He took his fishing knife from his belt and cut the anchor rope, leaving just sufficient for him to get a good grip on it. He had no idea what to do next. After a moment's thought, he decided to swim back to the beach pulling the boat behind him.

By this time, the tide was just about to turn. He found he was making no progress going to the shore but was being taken along the shoreline parallel to the beach in the 'easterly drift'. This is the name of the current which is prevalent along the south coast from the Southampton area to Dover.

All of a sudden, he saw the rock breakwater ahead of him and he knew that, if he continued on the present course, it would stop his advancing further. He could easily reach the beach by clambering along the rocks at the water's edge towing the boat behind him. Much to his surprise, this plan worked and he was soon back on dry land. He pulled the boat up the beach and took a look inside. The eel was very much alive and he could see that in its mouth was a whole small fish. It would seem that, while he was pulling up the anchor, he had hooked a pouting on his line. This was taken immediately by the large conger which had obviously been on the prowl looking for its next meal.

He really did not know what to do. Luckily, there were two professional fisherman by the rock formation. He hailed them to help him with his catch. They were amazed at the size of the conger. But they were used to dealing with large fish and they soon had the head removed. Although it seemed a funny thing to do at the time, they kept the head to enable them to weigh that as well when the eel was placed on the scales.

The fish measured 4'2" in length and weighed in at 32 lbs. The largest fish of any description that Pete had ever caught – and the largest conger caught off Folkestone for many a year.

While he was congratulating himself on his prize catch, he thought of Rob and Harry. What would they say about his conger? But, of course, they would have done much better on their trip out from Brixham. At least they would be dry when the boat they were on reached the beach.

Devon Ladies

The Johnson family was not that well off. Expensive flights to exotic holiday destinations were beyond their means. But this did not stop them holidaying abroad. It was just that they went by car and took with them their very large tent and all the other necessities attached to camping.

Camping enabled them to visit the most expensive resorts at purely nominal cost. After a few years, however, the excitement of erecting and dismantling a tent every three or four days wore a bit thin. It was decided that a caravan hooked on the back of their car might offer a good alternative.

They bought a 14' Cavalier caravan which was good to look at and most comfortable inside. It had its own kitchen and a separate toilet. But Les soon found that he did not exactly agree with the comments of the vendor that "You won't know you've got it on the back of your car." He found towing the caravan to be far from easy.

They had made a booking already on the ferry to take the car and caravan to the Continent for their summer holiday. But they felt that a mini-break in this country might get them more used to towing.

Accordingly, they decided to drive down to Devon. They stayed the first night on the Hog's Back close to Guildford and then proceeded onwards to Beer in Devon.

The local campsite at Beer was virtually full to over-flowing. The only space available was on a terribly steep slope which led down to the beach. But, having blocked the wheels, they enjoyed their first day there. Having walked down to the town to do some shopping, Tony and his son, Peter, passed the local church hall. Peter, seeing a sign which read 'Whist Drive Tonight - All Welcome' asked his father if whist was anything like the game of Bridge which they played together regularly. "Yes" replied Tony "It's very similar. The main difference is that you don't have to say in advance how many tricks you are going to win."

"Shall we have a go, Dad?"

"Yes, we'll give it a try if you like. What time did they say it started?"

"7.30 pm, Dad."

By this time they had arrived back at the campsite and Peter announced their plans to his mother and sister.

"It sounds a good idea to me, Tony." said Tony's wife, Mavis.

"Why don't you two go on your own while?" We'll be happy enough watching the television here in the caravan. We'll be fine."

Peter wandered down with his container to get some water from the communal tap. En route, he passed the time of day with the man in the next caravan to their own and, for something to say, told him of their planned trip that evening.

"Well," said his neighbour "I hope you have a good time but don't expect to win anything. Those Devon ladies are hot stuff at whist. They take with them the brown paper and string to wrap up the prizes."

"Thanks for the tip but we are experienced Bridge players so we should be able to hold our own."

Tony and Peter arrived early at the church hall and received the warmest of welcomes from the local ladies. On hearing that their visitors were new to Whist, they invited them to play a few practice hands with them before the formal start. Tony and Peter had some good cards and they played like Masters.

The lady in charge told the assembled group: "These two gentlemen from London play ever so well. They have just won every trick on the last hand. I think we shall enjoy having them with us this evening. Thank you very much for coming."

Tony and Pete smiled - which was just as well they did for that was the last smile they had the whole evening. One little old lady who had a two inches of ash on the end of the cigarette dangling from between her lips, knew every trick in the book. The lads didn't win a single game.

When the prizes were awarded at the end of the evening neither they nor any of the other visitors took a single prize. Even the booby prize for the worse play went to one of the Devon ladies.

"Just don't ask me about it" Peter said to his mother and sister on being asked how they had got on.

Tony and Peter both learnt a little more about how to play cards that evening.

Helping Out

"John, can I just drag you away for a few moments? I need your thoughts on a project we have in mind. As a Council, we have come up with an idea to attract new businesses to our area." These were the opening words of the Council's chief executive, Bob Meakins, when he met John Hawkins at a Council reception for local businessmen.

He continued "We are prepared to provide each business thinking of coming to the borough with setting-up finance to a maximum of £25,000. Security for the money would take the form of the Council holding shares in the business. If the average new firm were to take on four people, by the time we have collected business rates it should prove a good investment for us as well as helping them.

"My fellow councillors want to set up a Venture Capital Company and I would like very much for you to serve on the Board of Directors. It would be a registered charity, so you would automatically be a trustee of it as well.

"Frankly, we need somebody with your experience of business and knowledge of the locality. Could you help us out with that?"

John was honoured to be asked but was heavily involved with two new companies he had taken over.

"Well, it was very kind of you to think of me for this role but my available time is very limited. May I just ask who else is likely to be on the Board and what amount of time do you consider likely to be required each month?"

"Let me assure you John that you won't get lumbered with all the work. We have already appointed the Chairman of the Board. You will know him, he is David Fuller. We felt we needed a Chartered Accountant heading up the project. He will be joined by three other local businessmen Peter Jarvis, Harry Marchant and Tony Francis. I think you know those people - as well as the Council's representative, Jack Holmes. David thinks that one meeting each month of a couple of hours should suffice."

John was quite relieved because he knew the others led busy lives as well and represented the world's workers as opposed to paintings on the wall. He agreed to go along with the idea but, in his heart of hearts, the warning bells were already ringing. His experience had taught him to watch out when things look too easy.

He soon found the catch. The paperwork required to conform to the many legal requirements had to be seen to be believed. The whole thing was horrendously time-consuming. Still, he thought, once 'Bexley Venture Capital Company' was up and running, things should settle down quite quickly.

But other problems soon presented themselves. With many small businesses a £25,000 investment could represent for the smaller outfits a greater sum than that being put in by the owner of the business. This meant that the Council would hold considerably more shares in the company than the owner. This was a useless arrangement from everybody's point of view.

Another problem which soon became apparent was the Council's investment agreement. This consisted of some 245 pages of pure jargon and meant that solicitors had to be involved and their costs met.

After three months, the Council was concerned that none of the £250,000 deposited in the new Company's bank account had actually been allocated to a single business.

John pointed out over and over again that: "We are never going to be able to utilise the money until we have re-thought the project. We need to come up with something involving far less by way of legal expenses to start with. At the same time, we must find a way of permitting the owners of the business to retain more of the shares in their own company."

It became obvious to all that a complete change of direction was required. All, that is, apart from the current Chairman. He was having none of it. He was a stickler for the rules. "Nothing can be changed. We must be certain that the Council's interests are secure at all times." This was his stand whenever the other Board members wanted amendments. He was a very nice man and nobody wanted to offend him so they just let it ride.

The problem was resolved - but not in any way that anybody would have wished. The Chairman died.

The other Board members wanted John to take over the position. It was not that John would be better at the job than they would be; rather that they were more experienced than John at not getting lumbered with jobs they didn't want.

Almost immediately, the Board replaced the existing agreement with a document consisting of two pages of print. This was in everyday language which did not involve solicitors. In addition, instead of investing the £25,000 in the company, whatever sum was required up to that figure was loaned at a fixed rate of interest. The Council also purchased a 10% shareholding in the company concerned. There was no requirement to repay any of the capital in the first five years but the owners could choose to do so as and when they pleased. The interest charged was modest but even this was reduced by the ability of the owners to deduct tax before making payment.

The new format resulted in countless enquiries and, after two years, some seventeen new companies were brought into existence, employing around 75 people.

But it had turned out to be a full-time job for John and very time consuming for all the other Directors, who took on the role of mentors to the new companies.

After two years and completely out of the blue, the whole project ground to an abrupt halt when the Council decided to withdraw its funding. It announced also that the assistance of the existing team of businessmen as mentors was no longer required. This duty would be undertaken by the Council's own staff. Over the next three years, there was no mentoring but a great deal of monitoring resulting in the failure of sixteen of the seventeen companies formed.

All the members of the Board were thanked profusely for their work but they remained furious with the Council. What a waste of time and energy it had all been! But, more importantly, they saw potentially good businesses go to the wall for lack of sensible advice.

Six months passed and John received a letter from Bob Meakins asking him to go to lunch. At first he refused the invitation but Meakins phoned him and said: "My colleagues and I are so very sorry that, after all your hard work, the venture capital trust had to be wound up. We have our own ideas on these things but, following each election, we invariably have a new set of bosses who have different projects from the previous majority. There was nothing I could do. I'm so sorry, John. I would like to make it up to you."

John made it clear that he was not going to get involved with another fiasco like the last but the apology seemed so sincere that he reluctantly agreed to the lunch.

After lunch and a few glasses of wine, where the conversation was restricted to holidays and the like, Meakins said "Look, John, by way of compensation, we have come up with a fresh idea on which I would value your advice. Yes, I must confess that it is another project. But this time it is very different. You won't have to do any work but merely give the odd advice as required and I hope...."

"Oh, I don't think that I can take on anything at the moment" John interrupted. But Meakins continued: "We already have in mind a first class manager to run the thing, Frank Phillips. Although he has much experience in the industrial world generally, he is not too *au fait* with the way that Councils operate. We hoped that you would serve on the management committee to give guidance as and when necessary."

It was obvious from the look on John's face that he was far from sold on the idea. This prompted Meakins to add: "It might be helpful, John, if I just give you a quick run-down on what we have in mind. Basically, we have secured factory premises in the old Vickers' site at Crayford. We shall use these to train up to 114 unemployed school-leavers – most of whom will probably be either physically disabled or mentally fragile. I had you in mind, John, as I knew that your son had walking difficulties and I thought your input would be good all round.

"The training itself will take a very practical form. The helpers will be skilled painters, decorators, plumbers, carpenters and the like. Most of these will have been made redundant or will be of retirement age and looking for some way to put their skills to good use. Others will just want to put something back into the community."

John liked the sound of the scheme but wanted to see the manager and the factory before committing himself to the project.

Having done so, he readily agreed to be part of the management team which was chaired by a local councillor, who happened to be an exceptionally talented lady with business skills.

John took to the work immediately and soon started to really enjoy helping out. He could see youngsters, who might otherwise just be sitting at home watching the television, enjoying learning new skills. To see a lad in a wheelchair with a soldering iron in his hand working at a bench was a joy to behold. Between them, the kids seemed to be able to do almost anything. They even built a replica wooden canon for use on the village green.

Word of the scheme spread to neighbouring areas and children came from those to work at the factory. It was virtually a 'full house' every week. For John, it involved just an hour or two each month. But, to be truthful, he just popped his head round the door of the workshop whenever he was passing. The manager, Frank, was just great at the job. He filled everybody – trainers and trainees alike - with enthusiasm. This was what was needed.

There was always a buzz of activity. Often there was disappointment as each day came to an end. Without exception, everybody enjoyed working there and learning a trade. Of course, although small and not the objective of the scheme, the sale of goods helped towards the running costs. Some of the children were trained and engaged on the inevitable paperwork associated with any work. So, everybody was involved.

All went well until, without notice, the Council funding ceased abruptly and instructions came through that the factory would be closing at the end of the week.

"But what about the kids?" was the cry from everybody on the management team. There was no response at all to this and another truly worthwhile scheme bit the dust. It was later found that it was the Government who withdrew funding from the local authority for the project.

John decided that enough was enough. He was fed up to the back teeth with local authorities and spent all his free spare time raising money for the town's hospice.

Celtic Law

The year was AD51. Oroles and Robobostes were Celts - or 'Britons' as the Romans called them. One morning they were chatting to a couple of Roman legionaries called Diodorus and Antoninus from the local camp some ten miles from Londinium.

"Hi, guys. We're new here. We haven't seen many of your people before with your big bushy moustaches and not wearing skins. You can't be locals. Where are you from?" asked Antoninus.

"That's a long story. Shall I tell him or will you Robo?"

"You do it, Oro; you are better at these things than I am."

Oroles continued: "Well, we were born here but our ancestors came from central Europe just south of Switzerland. But I should say that we didn't get to Britain by invasion like your lot. I must confess that this was only because they couldn't agree on a couple of minor issues like: who would lead the army and, secondly, who would pay for it. So we settled for infiltration. That way everybody was relatively happy.

"You Romans just barge your way in with boat-loads of troops but I guess that's just your way of doing things. Mind you, you do make a lot of enemies the way you simply ship off as slaves some of those locals who won't join your army as auxiliaries. I'm not saying that we are perfect but we draw the line at that type of thing.

"I remember reading that, at one time, we had politico-military rule in parts of Transylvania but we settled for teaching them things like how to make specialised ironwork – ranging from helmets to funeral carts. We introduced such things as the potter's wheel. It was good for them and good for us."

Antoninus replied: "We all have different priorities, that's all. You go on about how clever you are but just take a look at the roads we have built linking your major towns. You would never have got round to doing that on your own, would you!"

"Probably not, because we always want to know who is going to pay for things like that. But I suppose the main problem we Brits have with you is we resent the fact that you put it about that we are all savages like Boudicca's lot. The other day, I heard one of your guys telling somebody that we were 'Kelts'. Well, as it happened, I learnt some Greek when I was at one of our universities here and that word comes from the Greek word 'Keltoi' – which means 'barbarians'. Just answer me this: How long have barbarians been making pendants, brooches, belts and buckles out of bronze, copper and silver?

"We adopted the teachings of Pythagoras donkeys' years ago and, when there are disputes between Europeans, we are almost invariably the first ones called on to act as arbitrators. I would remind you that we were minting silver coins a couple of centuries ago from our four mines in France. And I would bet my last penny that, if you had a choice between your own armour and ours, you wouldn't pick yours! Yet you tell everybody that we're barbarians. We know you do that as you don't like playing second best to the countries you invade.

The two Romans were a bit taken aback by this verbal attack because they only wanted to pass the time of day. Feelings were aroused and Antoninus came back angrily.

"Well, you obviously don't think much of us but what you do leaves a lot to be desired. To start with, you Brits are far too lenient on the villains. You need to follow our example with harsher penalties!"

"What? Throw them off the cliff or chuck them in jail, I suppose! You Romans hate our practice of fining people. You don't like the rich having to pay more for their crimes than the poor.

"We fine them a percentage of their income for each offence and not a set amount. So, if a guy breaks the law by driving too quickly in his chariot so as to be a danger to the public, we fine him 10% of his annual income. If he is poor, he pays little but, if he is rich, like some of your people, then he pays a lot.

"We regard this as being a fairer system. You must have more rich people to worry about than we do! Your local Legate is evidence of that – he must be absolutely loaded. Where did he get all that?"

Anton came back: "I'll ignore that last remark but tell me this: it's all right fining the villains but what happens when they don't pay? Answer me that, if you can!"

"Of course, some can't or won't pay fines" replied Oro, "In which case their families have to do so and the guy is ostracised and refused work until he coughs up. It has the added advantage, too, that parents keep a better watch on what their kids are doing. You need to remember that it's great chucking people in clink but who pays for them being there? The cost comes out of your pay packet at the end of the day!"

Anton shrugged his shoulders and said: "Well, I suppose that there is something in what you say but our system works – and, if the toy ain't broke......

"You've told us about your gripe; now let me tell you ours. You do nothing but moan about our invading your country but what you seem to forget is that it wasn't yours to start with – and the place would be empty by now if it were not for foreigners arriving all the time."

"Well, that may be so but it's all going to change. We're going to put a stop to all those foreigners arriving here by the boat-load. Mind you, it might take a bit of time."

Diodorus and Antoninus turned to go with Diodorus saying: "Oh, well. We'll see you around some time and by then you might have worked out how to stop all those foreigners coming here." They laughed and went on their way.

When the Romans were out of hearing distance, Oro turned to his friend and said: "You know, Robo, whatever that lot say, I think this system of ours is good and that it might well live on after we're dead and buried."

How right he was.

Nice Plaice

Alf and Ben were old workmates. Both were in their late fifties. Alf was a 'Man of Kent' and Ben a 'Kentish Man' although they only lived about a mile apart. This was because the title goes with whichever side of the River Medway that you were born. They could see each other's houses across the river.

They were talking one day at work.

"My goodness, Alf, you look well. Been out in the sun have you?"

"No, Ben, just doing a bit of fishing in the fresh air in the few days I had coming to me. As you know, I normally get bored stiff after only half a day if the fish aren't biting. But this last week I have had fish after fish and I just didn't want to do anything else but catch them."

"Well done. I've been fishing down at Dungeness by the power station a couple of times of an evening but the catch has been poor. Were you beach fishing or in a boat?"

"This was straight off the beach. I found a nice little spot that I hadn't tried before and the fish kept coming."

"Would you mind telling me where it was or are you going to keep that to yourself?"

"No, I don't mind telling you but to be quite to be quite honest, it was a little rocky area I had never tried before. On the Riviera."

"My goodness, that's sounds both posh and expensive. That must have cost you a bomb!"

"No, not really. I motored down with the wife and found a nice little place that did B & B. It was modest and very close to the Beach.

Nearly as cheap as going down and staying at Dungeness. The weather was nice and the wind was from the West – always a good sign. As you probably know, the old saying among fisherman is that 'Wind in the east the fish bite least. Wind from the west the fish bite best'. It was a long way but well worth the trip.

"Well, I'll be jiggered. I got week a due to me, too. I'll take that now and drive down myself. I could do with catching a few fish. Where exactly was it you went? Could you let me have some directions?"

You won't need those, Ben. The fishing's good all along that bit of the coast. Just drive along the main road and you will see plenty of small houses that advertise rooms. You can then fish anywhere you fancy. If you take a small garden fork with you, it's easy to dig a few worms in the sand at low water. But, funnily enough, you don't see many other anglers there."

The two men met up again ten days later.

"Well, Alf. I must have been unlucky but I found it a very long drive at my age. I was absolutely tired out by the time I got there. I don't know where you got 'terribly cheap' from; I found it all very expensive indeed – especially by the time I paid for the motorway toll. Coupled with that my wife doesn't like it too hot. And how would you believe that I hardly had a fish all week."

"Motorway toll? Too hot? Where on earth did you go then? I went down there again myself a couple of times last week; there was no charge on the motorway and the fish were still coming out."

Ben explained: "We got to this place close to Nice but it was too dear for us there, so we drove along to a little village just outside St. Maxime. That was too much really to pay but it was the best we could do. How come you found it so cheap?"

"What on earth are you talking about? It sounds to me that you have been all the way down to the south of France. The 'Riviera' I was talking about is between Folkestone and Sandgate! It's clearly marked as you drive along the main road and turn left at the bottom of Sandgate Hill. You must be crackers thinking I would go to the south of France, it's as much as I can do to drive from Chatham to Folkestone with my back. You know that, you daft monkey!"

"But you did say that it was a long way and it's not a long way to Sandgate."

"I was talking about the distance from the car park to the beach. You have to park your car in the picnic area and then walk with all your fishing gear the quarter of a mile down to the front. And I can tell you that it feels a lot farther coming back up the hill! I just can't start to believe that you drove all the way down to the south of France. I shall have to draw you a map the next time I suggest a fishing ground to you, otherwise Heaven alone knows where you'll finish up!"

Tim's Car

Tim Harris was 48 years of age. He had been with his employers for more years than he cared to remember. They manufactured innovative building tools and parts. He had risen through the various departments to become the company's' senior representative. He enjoyed a sales record which was the envy of all.

His lovely family appeared to be his sole interest in life. They all went out together to watch the local cricket or football teams play. They would swim in the sea near to where they lived at Eastbourne in the summer or in the local swimming pool during the colder months.

Indeed, his family, cricket and football were the main subjects of conversation when he visited his clients. He would open a conversation by asking such things as "How is young John liking his new school? It must be hard for him to be away from home for so long? Is your Mary fully recovered now from her op?" This immediately endeared him to his clients and talk about his company's products was in short supply.

Often the buyer was actually forced into asking Tim what new products were on offer and whether they were worth buying. Tim's reply would more often than not be along the lines of: "Well, we now have this new tool which measures water penetration. In all fairness, it does look particularly good but I would suggest that you hang on for the moment before ordering it. Just put a note in your diary to ask me about it in a month's time when I call again. All the initial problems - which are bound to arise with anything that new- will have been sorted."

In reality, this meant that Tim had an assured sale on his next visit. Any other representative calling after him offering the same type of equipment for immediate delivery would be shown the door. You could always rely on Tim to be honest with you on whatever you felt you needed. He would put you right.

As his area was quite large, Tim knocked up a fair old mileage in his company car. This was almost invariably one of the smaller Ford family cars on the market. His firm replaced it once a year with the latest model. So talk about his car was invariably also included somewhere in the conversation. He encouraged good humoured ribbing by his clients about its size and performance. One client always used to pull Tim's leg by saying things like: "I used to have Ford when I was poor!"

The relationships built over the years left his competitors out in the cold.

One day, Tim called to see a regular client and the conversation took its usual form. Until, that was, out of the blue, the client said to Tim: "I know you will forgive my saying so, but what on earth made you get a car that colour?"

Tim answered: "Well, the company buys the car and, to be perfectly honest, the only thing which is left to me is the actual colour. To add to the fun at home, we have this rule in the family that we each take it in turns to choose what colour it should be. This time, it was my five year old Peter's turn. As I've told you before, Peter is a smart little chap. He just loves fire engines so he picked this bright red one as the colour of our next car. So what could we do but go along with it?"

Much laughter all round but, of course, the car's colour was the subject of light-hearted conversation at each call that month for, if the client didn't mention it, Tim would say: "Just come to the window and see what young Peter has done to me now!"

The competition would have to get up early of a morning to beat Tim.

END OF STORIES

Write-up on Author

ROBERT NOTT *Msc, Diplomas in Advanced Psychology, Advanced Counselling, Criminal Psychology, Stress Management (PTSD) and TEFL.*

Index